Anonymous

The Crisis

Reflections on the proposed settlement of the British government

Anonymous

The Crisis
Reflections on the proposed settlement of the British government

ISBN/EAN: 9783337380960

Printed in Europe, USA, Canada, Australia, Japan

Cover: Foto ©Andreas Hilbeck / pixelio.de

More available books at **www.hansebooks.com**

THE

C R I S I S,

OR

REFLECTIONS

ON THE

PROPOSED SETTLEMENT

OF THE

BRITISH GOVERNMENT.

THE

CRISIS,

OR

REFLECTIONS

ON THE

PROPOSED SETTLEMENT

OF THE

BRITISH GOVERNMENT.

DUBLIN:

PRINTED BY P. BYRNE, No. 108, GRAFTON-STREET.

M,DCC,LXXXIX.

CRISIS, &c.

IN this ſtrange and eventful juncture, when ſubjects of the moſt anxious importance ſeize the general mind, and new queſtions of the greateſt magnitude, and moſt alarming conſequence, ſolicit our attention; I flatter myſelf I ſhall be excuſed for treſpaſſing on the public, with ſome reflections on the preſent ſtate of the *Britiſh* government, chiefly calculated for the meridian of this country. Whether a ſincere regard and tender attachment to our gracious ſovereign, or an outrageous ambition, and inſatiable thirſt of power has urged forward the conſideration of abſtract propoſitions, teeming with heat, and violence, and unreaſonable contention, it is not for me to ſay,

but

but of this I am confident, that were his
Majesty, with the eye of returning intellect
to look abroad, for a moment, and see the
wound which has been inflicted on the royal
prerogative, and the daring blow which
has been aimed at the title, by the lineal
descent of the crown, in his august line.; he
would shrink back with surprize and abhorrence ; but should he perceive that this
was done under the specious pretence of
affection to his person, and zeal for his in-
terests and those of the constitution, how
would his indignation rise against the
boldness and hypocrisy of such an attempt.

Speculative questions and abstract propo-
sitions, whether in religion or politics, are
observed to irritate and inflame men's paf-
fions the most violently, and excite the most
rancorous difputes, and outrageous animo-
sitics; a recent proof of this we may find,
in the heats which at this day are excited,
if I am not misinformed, in the fister kingdom, by the difcuffion of propofitions
important indeed, most highly important
in their subject, but abstract in their nature. It were to be wished for the sake
of the *Englifh nation*, that this difcuffion had not been obtruded on the public;
however as they are now brought forward,
and thrown before the people, it is become
necessary

neceſſary to conſider them, and if conſidered at all, they ſhould be conſidered with
a diligent, even with a ſolicitous and anxious
attention. The conſideration of theſe queſtions embraces the whole form of the Britiſh
conſtitution, and may produce the moſt de-
ciſive effects on the general repoſe and har-
mony, and permanency of the preſent eſtabliſhed government.

A little learning is a dangerous thing. I
am no more a friend to a haſty, jejune, and
popular diſcuſſion of great political queſtions,
than I would be to a ſimilar examination of
the tenets and myſteries of our religion;
the reſult in both caſes, will be errors in
principle and in practice. I have converſed
with many perſons on the momentous ſubjects, which now ſolicit our attention, and
been ſurprized to find among the genera-
lity, not excepting thoſe whoſe profeſſional
purſuits might lead them to form clear
and decided notions, on points of conſtitutional law, the utmoſt confuſion and incon-
ſiſtency; violent prejudices taking place of
principles, and ſtrong aſſertions ſubſtituted
for arguments. If the public prints do not
miſrepreſent the debates on ſome late occa-
ſions, the caſe is much the ſame in *England*,
every man is more ready to pronounce than
to enquire, and the form of the conſtitution
is loſt and diſappears amidſt the ſmoak and
miſt ariſing from party heat. That this
ſhould

fhould happen at fuch a junĉture, and when each individual is liable to be called on to give an account of the faith which is in him, is much to be lamented. I flatter myfelf he will not feem to deferve ill of his fellow citizens, who fhall offer to their confideration fuch refleĉtions and fentiments on the great national queftions before us, as a moderate attention to conftitutional principles, may fuggeft to a very humble capacity; after which I fhall beg leave to add a few remarks, which I think peculiarly offer themfelves to the the confideration of *Irifhmen.*

I proceed now, to confider Mr. Pitt's fecond Refolution.——*That it is the right and duty of the Lords fpiritual and temporal, and commons of Great Britain now affembled, and lawfully reprefenting all the eftates of the people of this realm; to provide the means of fupplying the defeĉt of the perfonal exercife of the royal authority, arifing from his Majefty's faid indifpofition, in fuch manner as the exigencies of the cafe may require.* I quote the refolution verbatim, becaufe I think almoft every word of it is material, and requires fome animadverfions. In the firft place, I think there is a fort of technical craft, a kind of artifice of fpecial pleading in the defcription of the affembly whofe right is to be declared; it is not fimply the Lords and Commons of Great Britain; nor the two eftates of parliament: expreffions

experffions which as the framer of the refolution knew would not ferve the turn, but
Lords and Commons now affembled and reprefenting all *the eftates of the people of this
Realm;* words that fupprefs the real ftate
of the fact, namely, that the two eftates of
Parliament did fimply meet purfuant to a
prorogation by the *King,* while in health ;
and hold out the *magnificent* but *unfounded,*
and *delufive idea,* of a *great National Convention, now* affembled, in fome extraordinary
manner, to anfwer the purpofe of the prefent emergency. I appeal to any man of
common candour, whether this be not the
obvious fenfe of the words; and whether
there is not here a fuppreffion of truth, a
fort of artifice and miftating highly unworthy
of the awful occafion, and of the folemnity
of national counfels. In the next place this
refolution takes for granted a propofition
which is not founded in fact, or at leaft
which ought to have been proved before it
was affumed as a corner ftone on which to
found a legiflative act. That the two Houfes
of Parliament, the Lords and Commons of
Great Britain, do *fully* reprefent all the
eftates of the people of the Realm—It is ea-
fier to affert than prove this propofition, as
I fhall obferve hereafter. Mr. Pitt found it
neceffary to the delufive idea of a convention, the principal fupport of the Refolution
before us; and being well aware that it was
queftionable

queftionable, flides it in artfully enough as part of a defcription : I fhall laftly obferve on the words, *in fuch manner as the exigencies of the cafe may require*, that they are much too lax and comprehenfive in their meaning to be defended on conftitutional grounds. In a Propofition of fuch vaft magnitude, and in a cafe fo new, there fhould have been the utmoft accuracy and precifion in the terms which were to declare a great and perhaps an eventful right; inftead of which, we have either a grofs inattention, or a ftudied and dangerous uncertainty. The words now before us, in their natural conftruction, and obvious import, make the two branches of the legiflature, in cafe of the King's indifpofition, arrogate to themfelves an arbitrary difcretion, and unlimited authority, not merely to elect or appoint a Regent to fill up the chafm, but abfolutely to difpofe of the executive power, to provide *ne quid detrimenti capiat refpublica.* So that under this Propofition, worded as it is, and literally taken, the two eftates would be warranted to fuperfede the King entirely, and to fubftitute for *Kingly*, any other form of government they might think proper. I muft add, that this Propofition makes the *Houfe of Commons* pronounce on the power of the *Houfe of Lords.*

So much for the form of Mr. Pitt's fecond Refolution; but to proceed to the real effence,

fence, the affertion that in cafe of difability through ficknefs of a King of *Great Britain*, who has an Heir Apparent of full age to govern and liable to no objection; the two remaining eftates of Parliament, have a right to elect any perfon they may think proper, as Regent during that difability, in prejudice to the claim of the Heir Apparent; or as it has been more ftrongly and concifely expreft, THAT THE PRINCE OF WALES HAS NO MORE RIGHT TO THE REGENCY THAN ANY OTHER SUBJECT IN THE KINGDOM; I hope to be able to demonftrate, that this Propofition has no foundation in *law* or any conftitutional principle; that it is not declaratory of any actual *exifting right*, there being none fuch; but is a change in the form of government, a *democratic innovation*, by arrogating to the two eftates of Parliament, newly created and before unheard of, powers.

I muft premife, that technical reafonings founded on our municipal law, and arguments drawn from analogy to the cafe of private property, do not apply to the fubject before us. Conftitutional cafes muft be governed by conftitutional principles; a certain vital fpirit of focial union, an informing effential purfuit of the public good, as the road to that is pointed out and defined by certain land marks or forms of political af-

B   fociation;

fociation. For inftance, the defcent of the Britifh crown is hereditary; the Heir Apparent fucceeds as of right on the demife of his predeceffor; yet is he but a truftee for his fubjects, the hereditary defcent of power is fubject to certain principles of conftitution; a tacit compact is underftood, that the Prince fhall employ his power for the good of his fubjects, and if he violates the truft he forfeits his crown. Now in the defcent of private property, there is no tacit compact underftood; the inheritor is not a truftee for his tenants; he is under a moral obligation indeed, but no pofitive one, to promote their good, nor will it, fhould he neglect or refufe to do fo, work a forfeiture of his eftate. A private individual it is faid can only become civilly dead in, two ways; a prince may become politically dead in as many ways as there are poffible violations of the original compact. No attainder of the heir of the crown, will bar the fucceffion to the throne, as it doth the defcent to a private perfon: the very defcent, by order of birth, will take away any fuch defect.

I proceed now to enquire, whether the two Houfes of Lords and Commons, in cafe of a temporary difability of the King, have, under the conftitution, an inherent right of appointing a Regent, to act in the name and

on

on the behalf of their fovereign, during his difability; and fhall afterwards offer fome arguments, to fhow, that it muft, under our conftitution, be incident to the ftation and rights of the Heir Apparent in cafe of fuch difability.

If the Lords and Commons, of the two Houfes of the Englifh Parliament, do really poffefs the power declared in the foregoing refolution, they muft be invefted with it, as a national convention, vertually comprehending the whole body of the people, all orders of the State; or elfe it muft be their right, as the two deliberate members of a legiflature, in which the executive power has a conftitutional affent and diffent.

I need not ufe many words, to prove that the Lords and Commons, in the two Houfes of Parliament, are not a national convention. A *national convention* is either an affembly of the whole aggregate of the people; or if their numbers render that impoffible, a full and adequate reprefentation, freely and impartially chofen, fo that every individual in the kingdom may give his fentiments directly, or indirectly, on the fubject of the meeting. But it will be not contended, that the Houfes of Parliament do fully and freely reprefent all the orders of the State. Mr. *Pitt* himfelf will not maintain this pofition; he who (though he was an enemy to that meafure in *Ireland*) fupported the plan for a parliamentary reform in *England*, and

B 2   thereby

thereby tacitly acknowledged, that the prefent House of Commons as it is now elected, i. not a full, fair, adequate reprefentation of the people.

Now to examine this claim of power, in the fecond point of view propofed. As power flows from the people, it muft purfue the channels, it muft preferve the form and diftinction marked out by the people. By them alone the conftitution may be recalled, or cancelled ; by them alone it can be altered and modified. If any one member of the State could itfelf affume a new power, or eftablifh an exclufive right, of defining and interpreting thofe already in exiftence, there would be a power in the conftitution not derived from the people. The two Houfes of Parliament, under the conftitution, have no power of legiflation either diftinct or conjointly ; they poffefs it only jointly, with each other, and with the King, the bond that holds them together is the King alone : they then form, as it were, a ftructure, where each part leans on each, and the whole is maintained, and upheld by a mutual preffure. They are a machine compofed of different wheels, each neceffary to a perfect and regular motion ; and if one be taken away the whole muft ftop or go wrong. But were the two Houfes of Parliament, in themfelves, to poffefs a right of fupplying the deficiency of the third Eftate,

that

that would imply a power of legiflation. If they appoint a certain power in the State, they muft arm that power properly, they muft ordain and enact a deference to its authority, elfe their appointment would be nugatory; and to do this they muft poffefs a legiflative authority. Mr. *Pitt* allows fuch an appointment to be an act of legiflation; for he fays, it muft be done by bill; and he allows, that the two Houfes of Parliament are incompetent to legiflate of themfelves; for he is obliged to refort to a fiction, and fet up a Pageant of Royalty, to give the act of thofe affemblies the form and validity of law; fo that his plan of proceeding is a refutation of his principle.

Every writer on *Englifh* law, who has treated this fubject, lays it down, that there can be no beginning of a Parliament, unlefs the King meets it either in perfon or by reprefentation; and that the affent of King, Lords and Commons, is neceffary to every Act of Parliament. A pofition folemnly recognized by the Act of the 13th of Car. 2, which declares that the Acts and Ordinances of the two Houfes, fhall not have the force of laws. Thefe reftrictions and limitations the conftitution hath wifely ordained, to preferve the executive power from the encroachments of the legiflative; and prevent the eftablifhment of tyranny by the union of both in the fame hands. " When (fays " *Montefquieu*,

" *Montesquieu*,)[*] when the legiflative and
" executive powers are united in the fame
" perfon, or fame body of magiftrates, there
" can be no liberty, becaufe apprehenfions
" may arife, left the fame monarch or fe-
" nate fhould enact tyrannical laws, to ex-
" ecute them in a tyrannical manner."—And
again. " But if there were no monarch,
" and the executive power fhould be com-
" mitted to a certain number of perfons fe-
" lected from the legiflative body, there
" would be an end then of liberty; by reafon,
" the two powers would be united, as the
" fame perfon would fometimes poffefs, and
" would be always able to poffefs a fhare
" in both;—Were the executive power not
" to have a right to reftrain the encroach-
" ments of the legiflative, the latter would
" become defpotic ; for as it might arrogate
" to itfelf what authority it pleafed, it
" would foon deftroy the other powers."

Thefe principles of Montefquieu are
adopted and enforced by Sir *William Blackftone*. The King, fays he, is the only branch
of the legiflature that has a feparate exiftence, or is capable of performing any act
when no Parliament is in being. Yet, by
Mr. *Pitt's* plan the other two branches of
the legiflature are declared to have a fepa-

* See Coke, 4 Inft. Hale of Parliaments, 1 Black.
Com. 153, Spirit of Laws, vol. 1. p. 221.

rate exiftence, are enabled to perform acts, and thofe of the utmoft moment. *" It is " highly neceffary for preferving the ba- " lance of the conftitution, that the execu- " tive power fhould be a branch, though not " the whole of the legiflature. The total " union of them would be productive of " tyranny: the total disjunction of them " for the prefent, would in the end, produce " the fame effects, by caufing that tyranny " againft which it feems to provide. The " legiflature would foon become tyran- " nical, by making continual encroachments, " and gradually affuming to itfelf the rights " of the executive power. Thus the long " Parliament of Charles the Firft, while it " acted in a conftitutional manner, with the " royal concurrence, redreffed many heavy " grievances, and eftablifhed many falutary " laws; but when the two Houfes affumed " the power of legiflation in exclufion of the " royal authority, they foon after affumed " likewife the reins of adminiftration, and " in confequence of thefe united powers, " overturned both Church and State, and " eftablifhed a worfe oppreffion than any " they pretended to remedy". If any en- croachments of the two Houfes of Par- liament, by fhaking off that conftitutional controul, excluding the royal *negative*, which

* 1 vol. p. 229, Com. 1. vol. p. 154.

like

like the *Veto* of *Roman* Tribunes, had not any power of doing wrong, but only of preventing wrong being done, and prefuming to legiflate without the concurrence of the crown, be fo formidable; muft it not be doubly formidable, as leading by a direct ard brief road to tyranny; when the propofed act of legiflation, in which the crown is to have no fhare, no power of rejection, purports no lefs, than to confer the poffeffion, modify the form, and prefcribe the extent of the executive power.

In whatfoever point of view we confider the refolution before us, it is irreconcileable to the principles of the conftitution. If the rights of Parliament are to be protected, on the one hand, the King is equally a part of the conftitutional government, the lineal defcent of the crown is equally neceffary to the public good, and therefore is equally eftablifhed by law; and the authority and prerogatives of the Sovereign, and the regular fucceffion to the throne of the reigning family, are to be guarded and maintained on the other hand; but the power attributed to the two eftates of Parliament is inconfiftent with the former, and may fatally endanger the latter.

If in cafe of an indifpofition of the King, abfenting him (as I may fay) from his place in the ftate, the heir apparent to the crown has no more right to the Regency than any

other

other subject, and the two Houses of Parliament have an exclusive right to supply the
deficiency of the personal exercise of the
royal authority; they must judge of the difability, they must absolutely decide on the
circumstance which suspends the personal
exercise of royal authority; they alone will
thus have an arbitrary power of declaring
that there is a deficiency of the executive
power, that is to say of superseding the King,
accompanied by an arbitrary power of filling
up the vacancy, by appointing a Regency or
or any other form of government in his
place, according as the exigency of the case, of
which exigency they themselves are to
be the sole judges, may demand. Thus will
the King become a tenant at will, wholly
dependent on the two Houses of Parliament,
and owe his existence and political stability,
not to the principles of the constitution, but
to the curtesy and forbearance of his legislative masters.

But supposing that the two branches of
the legislative power have an exclusive right
to provide for the deficiency of the executive as they shall think meet: who shall
compel them to exercise their function? if
they refuse to do so, must the executive
power become extinct? suppose this deficiency
to happen, at a time when the lower House
of Parliament is not in being, when a dissolu-
tion has taken place, and no writs have yet

C

been

been iſſued to call together a new Houſe of Commons; is the executive power to be ſuſpended and anarchy to prevail during the period of a long diſability? Perhaps the courſe of a long life? but the two Houſes of Parliament have a right of providing for the event, as they think proper, according to the exigencies of the caſe; ſuppoſe they ſhould vote that the exigencies of the caſe require that they ſhould aſſume it to themſelves, and ſo eſtabliſh an ariſtocracy, or ſome other Republican form of government.

If the Britiſh crown was made hereditary, it was not for the honour of a particular family or individual, it was from motives of convenience and public utility. The ſame principle, the ſame regard to the general weal demands that the perſonal exerciſe of the royal power ſhould be hereditary. Every argument drawn from a proſpect of the violent diſorders, from an apprehenſion of the civil diſcord, the furious commotions and fatal anarchy, that vex and debilitate States, when an elective monarchy prevails, may be applied to the caſe of a Regency. Indeed the principles of the reſolution before us, if duly followed up, ought to make the crown itſelf elective; for if the two Houſes of Parliament poſſeſſed the ſuppoſed right where the King is removed for a time only by indiſpoſition; ought they not, by a parity of reaſoning, to poſſeſs it, where the
King

King is wholly removed by a demife? I own I cannot fee any reafon, why they fhould be invefted with it, in the one cafe, and want it, in the other. It may be faid the fuccef-fion is fixed by ftatute; fo that my argument does not apply : but fo is the power of the two Houfes of Parliament fixed and defined by ftatute; but what are ftatutes oppofed to venerable precedents! the precedent of an elective Regency may very eafily be applied at a future day, to authorife an elective mo-narchy, and as the Houfes affume to them-felves the power of legiflation, though a fta-tute has declared that their acts fhall not have the authority of law; fo they may arro-gate to themfelves the power of appointing a King; though a ftatute has fettled the fuc-ceffion of the crown.

I know not, in political efficacy, the diffe-rence between an elective monarchy, and an elective executive power; and the two Houfes of Parliament, judging of the difabi-lity, and exclufively competent to fupply the deficiency of their King, might find it ex-pedient to fuperfede his authority, and ap-point elective Regents from father to fon in *Secula Seculorum.* The very *Sanity* of the King under this refolution becomes the fub-ject of party : he will derive the conti-nuance of his intellects, not from God and nature, but from the fufferance of popular demagogues and parliamentary leaders. A

factious

factious minifter, with the two Houfes of
Lords and Commons at his devotion, may
tyranize over his mafters houfe, may incapi-
citate his fovereign, fupply the perfonal exercife of his authority with creatures of his
own, in exclufion of the heir apparent; may
continue the difability through a long life,
and thus, under the name of a Regency, revive in *England* the antient government of
the *Mayors de Palais* of *France*, during fuch
an *interregnum*, for fo I may call it. An ambitious fubject, confpiring with the two legi
flative bodies, and aided by the influence of
the crown, might fortify himfelf in his poft
of eminence, might take fuch meafures, as
would render the return of the rightful heir
to the throne of his anceftors arduous or impoffible. Nor let this be thought a vifionary
fear; our anceftors would have thought an
apprehenfion of what is paffing before our
eyes, at this moment, equally vifionary.

Abftracted from thefe well-grounded fears;
obferve what monftrous abfurdities muft
flow, from the doctrine, which thus makes
the office of Regent elective. The appointment is to be made by Lords and Commons,
fays Mr. *Pitt*: but who fhall oblige the
Lords and Commons to co-operate, and concur in the defignation of a perfon, or the
defcription of his powers? they differed at
the time of the revolution, and the Lords
were with difficulty induced to yield to
the

the Commons. Each affembly is in-dependent of the other; they have no connection, no political unity in the ab-fence of the King; he is the great luminary that harmonizes their courfes, and holds them together in one fyftem. In their pre-fent fituation the Lords have no more connection, no more political co-exiftence with the Commons of Parliament, than with the Common Council of London. If the Lords and Commons differ, which fhall predominate? to what moderator of their difputes, what arbiter of their difference fhall they appeal? There may be one Re-gent for England appointed by the Lords, another by the Commons: their act will not, on any principle that I know of, be binding on *Scotland*, fo a third Regent may be chofen by the ftates of that kingdom. The act of the *Britifh Lords* and Commons has no force or validity to bind *Ireland*; each of the two Houfes of Parliament here, may choofe a Regent: thus will there be no lefs that *five Regents* of the Britifh Empire, all indepen-dent of each other; co-ordinate and confti-tutional. And, to add to the melancholy of fuch an event, as the indifpofition of the So-vereign; the country may be torn with dif-cord, and every appointment of a Regent be a trial of party ftrength.

All the advocates for the refolutions un-der our confideration, have been guilty of

an unpardonable fallacy, a fallacy, which is
no lefs than treafon againlt the conflitution,
and wholly confounds and outrages all our
legal ideas of kingly power, on the one
hand, a 'd the rights of the people, on the
other. They have affected to confider the
Lords and Commons, of the two Houfes of
Parliament, as the people, as the whole body
of the nation ; and dared to apply to them
the precedents of the Convention Parliaments, and the principles of the *reftoration*
and *glorious revolution.* And the relolution,
as I have already obferved, is very artiul-
ly couched in terms borrowed from the bill
of rights, that are applicabie to the whole
body of the people, and calculated to miflead
us, by the delufive notion.

Moft of the arguments advanced in fupport of thefe refolutions would be incontro
vertible, if applied to the nation at large, or
to a National Convention, and not to the two
Houfes of Parliament. They apply to
cafes where the neceffity is fuch as fuperfedes the forms of the Conftitution, not fuch,
as may be provided for, under the forms of
the Conftitution.

The power of the reprefentatives and the
people are widely different, and ought ever
to be kept diftinct ; if we mean to preferve
the power of the crown, and the rights of the
people. It will lead to the moft fatal confe-
quences, if we apply to the two *Houfes of Parliament,*

liament, the maxims and principles, which are true only, with regard to the great body of the people. The power of the PEOPLE is paramount to the Conftitution, and fuppofes a fufpenfion of it. The power of *reprefentatives* is according to the *conflitution*, and fuppofes it exifting. The power of the PEOPLE fuperfedes, regenerates, or creates the law. The power of *reprefentatives* is derived from, fubordinate to, maintained and defined by the law. The power of the PEOPLE is primary and abfolute; that of reprefentatives delegated and circumfcribed. The power of the PEOPLE fuppofes a deficiency of the crown, a vacancy of the throne, from whatever caufe. The power of *reprefentatives* implies a King filling the throne, exercifing the power, and performing the functions of royalty. Let it no more be faid therefore that Mr. *Pitt* afferts the caufe of liberty, that he vindicates the rights of the people. Such opinions can only originate with a profound ignorance of the Conftitution. Mr. *Pitt's* doctrines have the direct oppofite tendency; they would go to *annihilate the rights of the people, and abforb them in the devouring claims of an ariftocracy.*

The friends of Mr. Pitt's Refolutions will tell us, that precedents have been laid before them, to warrant the claim of the two eftates of Parliament, to a right of appointing the Regent, on fuch melancholy occafions cations as the prefent. Were any thing wanting to ftigmatize the weaknefs of their caufe, it would be their production of fuch precedents, and reliance on them as an authority. They have not been afhamed to refort to times of barbarity and confufion, to the fanguinary and miferable periods that ftain the page of hiftory, and while we read, make us fhrink back with abhorrence, and blufh to think we are men. What fhall we fay of the caufe, that can refort for a juftification to the examples of the bold ufurpation of the line of *Lancafter*, or the vindictive fury of the houfe of *York ?* What fhall we fay of thofe who will quit the fteady lights of law and conftitution, to guide themfelves by the faint dawning, and twilight of thofe days when mens minds were rude and unformed as the conftitution, when *the ftill voice of law and reafon was unheard;*[*] violence was the meafure of right, and every ufurper came to the Senate Houfe recking with blood, and there found an obfequious Parliament waiting to give the form and fanctions of law to the decifions of the fword! " The ancient hiftory of England " (fays Hume) [†] is nothing, but a catalogue " of reverfals and attainders; every thing is " in fluctuation and movement, one faction " is perpetually undoing, what was eftab- " lifhed by another; and the multiplied

---

[*] See Fofter's Crown Law, 398. Difcourfe 4th.
[†] Vol. iii, pa. 29.

" oaths,

' oaths, that each party required for the
' fecurity of the prefent acts, betray a per-
' petual confcioufnefs of their inftability."
The learned judge *Fofter* obferves, " that
" our hiftory furnifhes inftances, more than
" enough, of an unwarrantable revenge taken
" by the prevai ing faction ; that none of
" the attainders of thofe times, ought to be
" confidered as cafes from which the prin-
" ciples of the law can be deduced," and
adds from lord Hale,† " that Parliaments
" have always been obfequeous enough to
" the victor, and ready to pafs attainders
" for his fafety and their own."

Shall then the precedents of thofe times,
which in the opinion of our beft legal wri-
ters, cannot furnifh principles of law ; be
fufficient to eftablifh, what is ftill more important, principles of the conftitution? Municipal law is a lefs complex thing than
conftitution, the bulwarks of civil liberty,
and the bounds of perfonal fecurity are the
firft object; they are in fome degree underftood and fixed, before the functions of the
legiflature are defined, the balance of the
different orders of the ftate adjufted. Yet in
thofe days even law and jurifprudence were
imperfect, the precedents of the time would

---

* If the reader has any doubt on this fubject, he may
fatisfy himfelf by confulting the hiftory of thofe times ; and
he will find inftances enough in Hale's hiftory of the Pleas
of the Crown ; where he treats of treafon.

not

not now be received in our courts of juftice;
and leaft of all would be precedents of parliamentary attainders. If then the precedents of Parliament would be of no authority, or weight, where a fingle individual of
the meaneft rank ftood upon his trial; are
they to be decifive, in a meafure that involves the dignity, the welfare, perhaps the
peace and fecurity of a whole Empire?

We may judge what the parliamentary
precedents of thofe days are, fince we find,
in the reign of Edward II. and others fubfequent, the King perpetually iffuing his
ordinances, and iffuing them in vain, againft
the illegal practice, which prevailed univerfally among the great Barons, of coming to
Parliament, attended by large bodies of armed men;* and we find, in *Ryley*, a precedent of folemn treaty of peace, under the
mediation of the Pope's legate, between King
Edward II. and fome of his rebellious fubjects.

To illuftrate the foregoing general obfervations, by a few brief references to the
hiftory of the time. In the reign of Edward
II. from whence the firft precedent is taken,
the Barons having come to Parliament in
defiance of the laws and the King's prohibition, with a numerous retinue of armed

---

* See feveral inftances of thefe ordinances, in Ryley's
Placita Parliamentaria. Pla. Par. 538.

followers;

followers; that unhappy prince was obliged to fign a commiffion, empowering the Prelates and Barons to elect twelve perfons, with authority (which was to continue irrevocable till Michaelmas next) to enact ordinances for the government of the kingdom, and regulation of the King's houfhold, which fhould have all the force of laws and ftatutes.

We find the *Spenfers* attainted, that attainder reverfed, and again renewed by the Parliament of that time; we find thofe noblemen condemned to an ignominious death by the rebellious Barons, without even the form of a legal trial; we find that Parliament proceeded to try and depofe their fovereign, and renounced their allegiance to him by a folemn deputation; we find the King in the power of his rebellious fubjects, compelled by Durefs, to fign a refignation of the crown, and afterwards cruelly murdered by his own fervants at the inftigation of his neareft connexions. What weight or credit is given to the precedent of Parliament appointing a council of Regency to affift the young King? is it of more validity, than that by which *Mortimer* was condemned unheard, and which was afterwards reverft as illegal by a fubfequent Parliament? The precedents of thofe times would prove too much, we cannot pick and chufe from among them, they muft either

be

be received in *toto*, or all together repro-
bated.

Should we refort to the reign of Richard
II. we fhall find a precedent to fhew that
the Houfe of Lords alone poffeft the exclufive power of appointing perfons to exercife the executive power, in cafe of infancy
or incapacity of the King. The Commons
apply by petition, (which is remarkable)
to the Lords, and requeft them to appoint a
Council to manage public bufinefs ; and the
Lords do accordingly of their own mere authority appoint, not indeed a Regency, but
a Council of nine. But what Principles can
be collected from the tranfactions of a reign
that fets all principles legal or conftitutional
at defiance ? A Council of fourteen was appointed by the factious Barons, the commiffion to thofe perfons, ratified by Parlia
ment, all the power executive and legiflative transferred to them for a year, and the
King himfelf by violence compelled to fign
this commiffion, and fwear to the obfer-
vance of it. Five great lords accufed or
(as it was then called) appealed the King's
Minifters before Parliament, and Parliament,
who ought to have been the judges, bound
all their members, by an oath, to live and
die, with the lords appellants, and defend
them with their lives and fortunes. We
find Parliament condemning numbers of
their own body, without trial or examination,

on, to gratify the turbulent *Gloucester* and his faction; we find them condemning one of their own members to die as *a traitor*, to gratify the King, and this for no greater offence, than using the privilege of Parliament, and complaining in a debate among themselves, that the King's court was crouded with *Bishops and Ladies.* * In this reign the *Judges* of the land declared it as the law, " That the King hath the governance, and " may appoint what shall be first handled, " and so gradually what next in all matters " to be treated of in Parliament, even to " the end of the Parliament: and if any " person shall act contrary to the King's " pleasure made known herein, they are to " be punished as traitors." And that the Lords and Commons cannot, without the will of the King, impeach in Parliament, any of his judges or officers, for any of their offences; and if any one should so do, he is to be punished as a traitor. At the next Parliament (says Foster, a censure sufficiently severe and not warranted by any known rule of law did pass upon them, their own measure was meted out to them; but in the 21st of the King these questions with the judges answers, having been read in full Parliament, it was demanded of all the estates

---

* One Haxey who proposed some Petitions on the state of the nation.

of Parliament, how they thought of the anfwers aforefaid; and they faid, " *they thought*
" *the faid juftices made and gave their anfwers,*
" *as good and lawful liege people of the King*
" *ought to do."* " A Parliament (fays Fofter)*
" that could folemnly adopt principles, fo
" contrary to the whole tenor of the ftatute
" of treafons, anti-conftitutional in every
" point of view, fubverfive of the undoubt-
" ed rights of Parliament, and of all free-
" dom of debate in either Houfe, fuch a
" Parliament muft, unlefs under actual force,
" be the willing tools of defpotic power, and
" in either cafe its opinion deferves no man-
" ner of regard." This Parliament annulled,
for ever, the commiffion which had been
ratified by a former Parliament, and declared it treafonable to attempt, in future,
to revive a fimilar commiffion; abrogated
the acts that attainted the King's minifters,
declared the general pardon granted by the
King invalidas, extorted by force, and attainted the Barons who had oppofed the
King, and reverfed the attainder of *Trefi-*
lian and the other judges : but, what is very remarkable, this Parliament elected twelve
Lords and fix Commons to finifh all bufinefs which had been laid before *Parliament*
and not concluded, a proceeding which
alone fhould be decifive to fhew what cre-

* Fofter's C. L. 396.

dit

dit is due to the parliamentary precedents of this time.*

Come we now to the precedent of the acceffion of Henry IV: a precedent anulled by the act of Edward IV. revived by the 1ft of Henry VII. and which was more relied on than it deferved in the debates of the convention in 1688. The Duke of *Lancafter* called a Parliament in the King's name, he extorted a refignation of the crown from *Richard*, but unwilling to truft to that, he determined to have him folemnly depofed in Parliament; he drew up a charge of thirty-three articles againft him, and prefented it, to that body; it was not canvaffed, nor examined, nor difputed, in either Houfe, but feemed to be received with univerfal approbation. One man alone, the Bifhop cf *Carlifle*, had the courage to appear in defence of his unhappy mafter; and he was feized and imprifoned, by order of the Duke of Lancafter, for only delivering his fentiments in his place. Thus, we find Parliament claiming mighty powers, yet wanting every thing neceffary to them, even common freedom of debate. Thirty-three long articles of charge were at one meeting voted unanimoufly againft *Richard* by the fame Peers and

---

* In the reign of Edward III. there is a ftrange tranf-action; the trial of Sir Thomas Berkley in Parliament by a petty jury. Fofter's C. L. 387.

Prelates.

Prelates, who, but a little before, had vo-
luntarily and unanimously authorifed thofe
very acts of violence, of which they now
complained ; and the throne being vacant
by the depofition of *Richard*, *Henry* claimed it in the name of Father, Son, and Ho-
ly Ghoft, by the jumbled and inexplicable
title of Conqueft and Decent conjointly. He
did not refort to Parliament, as having the
power of appointing, but only of rocoghizing
the Sovereign ; he became King, nobody
could tell why or how, (except by force)
and the title of the Houfe of *March*,
which had formerly been recognized by
Parliament, was neither invalidated nor
repealed, but paft over in total filence.*

But fuppofing the precedents of the depofition of Edward II. and Richard II. were
conftitutional and legal ; they proceeded,
on a principle, which furely does not apply
to the cafe before us ; on the principle of
felf-defence, and a violation of the original
compact. Both thefe unhappy Princes were
fuperfeded for incapacity and malverfation ;
the principle was right, though the particular applications of it might be villainous.
If the charges were well founded, the conftitution was fubverted, the power had returned to the people ; and they were entitled
to interfere by the fame right of felf-defence,

* See Hume's Hift. England.

which

which nature gives, to nations as well as individuals, in cafes of neceffity.

Parliament, it is true, on the acceffion of Henry the 6th, which is the next precedent, took upon themfelves to fet afide the defignation of his father, who had by will, (which fhews that thefe exclufive claims of Parliament were not then recognized) appointed the Duke of *Bedford* Regent of France, the Duke of *Gloucefter* Regent of *England*, and committed the cuftody of the King's perfon to the Earl of *Warwick*; Parliament declined the name of Regent altogether, and appointed the Duke of *Bedford* Protector or Guardian of the kingdom, a title which they fuppofed to imply lefs authority; they invefted the Duke of *Gloucefter* with the fame dignity, during the abfence of his eldeft brother; in order to limit the power of both thefe Princes, they appointed a Council of Regency; and committed the cuftody of the infant King's perfon to his great uncle *Beaufort*, Bifhop of Winchefter, who, as his family could never have any pretenfions to the crown, might fafely, they thought, be entrufted with that important charge. This precedent, if it proves any thing, proves too much; but it proves nothing; it paft *fub filentio* through the moderation of the King's uncles, who acquiefced in what they probably did not approve. They were alone aggrieved, alone compe-

E.   tent

tent to call in queſtion, what had been done ; they knew the title of their nephew was diſputed, they ſaw the country involved in the greateſt war in which ſhe ever had been engaged; and ſubmitted, from prudential motives, to what they knew at the time to be a uſurpation, but knew alſo to be dictated by zeal for the King's perſon and government.

We come now to the other precedent of this reign on which Mr. *Pitt*, and the advocates for his reſolutions, have ſo ſtrongly relied; although they, and every body who looks into the hiſtory of that period, muſt be ſenſible, that this very Parliament, would inſtead of appointing York protector with limitted powers, have placed the crown at once on his head, had he been diſpoſed to take ſuch a decided ſtep. It is not in the principles of the conſtitution, as they were underſtood and laid down at that time; in the powers of Parliament as they were then defined ; or in the Duke of *York's* ſuppoſed deference to them ; that we are to look for a key to the precedent before us; but in the peculiar character of *Richard*, and the nice and peculiar circumſtances in which he ſtood. *York* was as much deficient in political, as he excelled in perſonal courage: though the crown was perpetually within his graſp, he feared to ſeize, what he wiſhed to poſſeſs. The Houſe of *York* had the beſt title, but
Henry

Henry the 6th had been in poffeffion of the crown almoft forty years by lineal defcent, and under a parliamentary fettlement, in which the whole nation had acquiefced, and his title was fupported by a numerous and powerful party. Thefe confideration intimidated *Richard*, and threw an appearance of inconfiftency over the refolves of thofe Parliaments, which were at his devotion. *York* demands redrefs of grievances at the Head of 10,000 men ; he difbands his army and flies, he returns, and the King being feized with an indifpofition, the Queen and Council are obliged to appoint him Lieutenant of the kingdom with power to fummon a Parliament ; and that Parliament appointed him Protector during pleafure. Here is a precedent of the Queen and Council of themfelves difpofing of the fupreme executive power, during the indifpofition of the King. Whether the name is Regent or Lieutenant the thing is the fame.

But it is faid Parliament impofed reftrictions on *York*, and therefore, here is a precedent of the power of Parliament. No, we muft look for thefe reftrictions in the exceffive caution of *York*, not in the power of Parliament ; he himfelf not Parliament impofed them ; a Parliament which entrufted the royal authority to a man, who had appeared in arms againft his Sovereign, and had fuch ftrong adverfe pretenfions to

cro-

crown, could not be averfe from his taking
poffeffion of it. Immediately after this
boafted precedent, we find the Houfe of
Peers alone affuming to themfelves the
fame powers, and actually exercifing the
fame functions, which, it is contended, the
preceding tranfaction gives to the *two Eftates
of Parliament*. The Houfe of Lords alone
annul the former appointment, and declare
the King to be reinfiated in his authority.
Can we find the feeds of the conftitution?
Can we difcover any rule of legal conduct
in fuch precedents as thefe? No, we find
only the rude viciffitudes of faction, and the
blind fubmiffion of Parliament, that common
engine of violence and wrong, to the pre-
vailing party.

After gaining the battle of *Northampton*,
and when the crown was within his grafp,
York, inftead of putting it on his head at
once, laid his title before the Houfe of Peers;
appealed to them as judges, and demanded
the Sovereign authority as his right from
their judicial determination. The Peers
take, as their affeffors, fome of the Commons;
and with that ufual regard to law and common fenfe, which marks the precedents of
thofe times, recognize the title of *Richard*;
but decree, that, as *Henry* had fo long ufurp-
ed the name of King, he fhould retain it
during his life, while *York* fhould poffefs
the whole exercife of the executive power;
that

that the latter fhould be acknowledged heir to the crown ; that every one fhould fwear to maintain his fucceffion; and that it 'fhould be treafon to attempt his life.

The acceffion of *Edward* the 4th to the crown is an inftance of a military election. The army was affembled, the croud being afked whether they would have *Henry* for King rejected him, the young Duke of *York* being then propofed to them, was received with loud acclamations; a number of Lords, Bifhops, and Magiftrates were next affembled, at Baynard's Caftle; they ratified the popular election ; and fo *Edward* became King. The firft Parliament called by him, declared all the Parliaments held under the Houfe of *Lancafter* illegal; and attainted King Henry the 6th, his Queen, and their adherents. About ten years after, that Pageant of a King *Henry* the 6th was reftored; all the Acts made in the Parliaments of *Edward* the 4th were repealed ; the Duke of *York* was declared an ufurper ; he and his adherents attainted ; and the attainders of the *Lancafter* party reverfed. But, a few months after, *Edward* prevailed over his enemies; and a Parliament was fummoned, which ratified, as ufual, all the acts of the victor, and recognized his authority.*

* Martial law was introduced at this time, and many of the nobility executed under it. The Conftable of England was authorized by his Commiffion, to proceed fummarie, and de plano, fine refpectu and figura juftitie fola facti veritate confpecta.

A precedent

A precedent was quoted, in debate, by Lord *Camden*, and with some appearance of triumph; but surely it need only be stated, to shew, that it does not apply to the present case. It was a determination of the *Lords Spiritual and Temporal* on a *Point* of *Law*; not an interference of the *two Houses* to appoint a *Regent*; and they decided the point of law properly. The point was this, the Duke of *Gloucester*, uncle to Henry the 6th, claimed, a right to *be Regent*, during the minority of his nephew, and in the absence of the Duke of *Bedford* his elder brother, who was nearer to the Throne; and they declare, that such desire was not caused nor grounded in precedent, nor in the law of the land. But is this an authority, to shew that the *Heir Apparent to the crown being of full age and ability, to govern, and present on the spot, has no more right to be appointed Regent than any other subject.* Precedents to shew, that the *presumptive* heir, has no right to the *Regency*, do not apply to the case of an *Heir Apparent*. Though Lord *Camden* will not suffer himself to suppose any difference between them, the law of *England* makes a wide one. The Heir Apparent who carries on the lineal succession, is more dignified, more highly favoured, in consideration of law. For proof of this, I shall only refer you to the Statute of Treason, [25 Edw. III.] which guards his person, with the

the fame eafe, as that of the King; and is equally folicitous to preferve the purity of his marriage-bed; a folicitude which is not extended to the heir prefumptive.

The conventions which reftored Charles the Second, and effected the glorious Revolution of 1688, do not furnifh any precedent to juftify the claim of the Lords and Commons to appoint a Regent. The power of thofe affemblies ftood on the peculiar circumftances of the time, their interference was warranted by ftrong neceffity. We cannot reafon from that interference, unlefs we are able to fhew that a like neceffity exifts at this day.

The true principles of- thofe two great events are put in fo clear a light by an admirable man and fincere friend of the conftitution, *Sir Jofeph Jekyl,* who was one of the managers for the Commons at *Sacheverell*'s trial, that I fhall tranfcribe fome of his words.——" It is far from the intent of " the Commons to ftate the limits and " bounds of the fubject's fubmiffion to the " fovereign; that which the law hath been " wifely filent in, the Commons defire to be " filent in too; nor will they put any cafe " of a juftifiable refiftance but that of the " Revolution only." And again, " To make " out the juftice of the Revolution, it may " be laid down, that as the law is the only " meafure of the Prince's authority and the " people's

" people's fubjection, fo the law derives its
" being and efficacy from common confent;
" and to place it on any other foundation,
" is to take away the obligation: this notion
" of common confent impofes on both prince
" and people, to obferve the laws."—" No-
" thing is plainer, than that the people have
" a right to the laws and the conftitution;
" this right the nation hath afferted, and
" recovered out of the hands of them who
" had difpoffeffed them of it, at feveral
" times. There are of this two famous in-
" ftances, I mean the *Reftauration*, and the
" *Revolution*; in both thefe great events,
" were the regal power and the rights of the
" people recovered."—" That the conftitu-
" tion was wholly loft, and recovered, at the
" Reftauration, is known to all. And be-
" fore the Revolution, it is known how
" Popery and arbitrary power had invaded
" the conftitution. The royal fupremacy, of
" fuch abfolute neceffity to preferve the peace
" of the kingdom, was difclaimed; the pa-
" pal fupremacy, by a folemn embaffy to
" Rome, acknowledged. At that time the
" popular rights in almoft all the fpecies
" were invaded; that great privilege of the
" people, on which all others depend, that
" of giving their confent to the making
" new or repealing old laws was invaded;
" and a difpenfing power, which rendered
" all our laws precarious, and at the will of
" the

" the Prince, exercifed. Thefe and a great
" many other acts of abfolute power, are
" mentioned in that act of Parliament called
" the *Bill of Rights*."—" And as the nation
" joined, in their judgment of their difeafe,
" fo they did in the remedy. They faw
" there was no remedy left but the laft, and
" when that remedy took place, the whole
" frame of the government was reftored en-
" tire and unhurt." †

The Parliament which reftored Charles,
being fummoned without the King's confent, received at firft only the title of *Con
vention*. And it was not, till the King paffed
an act for that purpofe, that they were called
by the appellation of *Parliament*.

What was done by the Convention of
1688, if duly confidered, will be found a
precedent, that inftead of fupporting the
claims of the Convention of 1788, militates
againft them. The Peers and Bifhops had
addreffed the *Prince* of *Orange*, defiring him
to fummon a *Convention*, by circular letters ;
and to affume in the mean time the manage-
ment of public affairs. All the members,
who had fat in the Houfe of Commons during any Parliament of Charles the Second,
(the only Parliaments whofe election was regarded as free) were invited to meet ; and
to them were added the mayor, and fifty of

† State Trials, V. 5. p. 667, 668.

the common council. This (fays Hume †)
was regarded as the moft proper reprefenta-
tive of the people, which could be fummoned
during the prefent emergence. They unanimoufly voted the fame addrefs, with the
Lords; and the Prince, being thus fupported
by all the legal authority, which could poffibly be obtained in this critical juncture,
wrote circular letters to the counties and cor-
porations of *England*; and his orders were
univerfally complied with.——A *Co·vention*
fummoned in this extraordinary way, and
returned by the people, in full contemplation of the great Revolution then depending,
and with full powers, and for the exprefs
purpofe, of fettling the government, cannot
furely be compared, with the Houfe of Commons returned under the King's writ, and
meeting, at a certain day, under the King's
prorogation; any more, than a temporary
indifpofition of the chief magiftrate, can be
compared with a total fubverfion of law and
conftitution. Amidft all the violence of party,
amidft the wildnefs of fpeculation, which
might have be enexcufable at fuch an extraordinary crifis, the *Convention* never dream-
ed of fuch claims, as have been advanced on
a late occafion. Amidft a convulfion, which
fhook the ftate to its bafe, they, with a pious
hand, collected and preferved the feeds of

the

the conftitution, from amongft the ruins.—
Even the moft zealous *Whigs* deprecated the
idea of making the Crown clective. They
grounded themfelves entirely on neceffity;
they confidered the cafe of the Revolution as
fingle and ifolated. They refolve, " That
" the King, by having endeavoured to fub-
" vert the conftitution; by violating the ori-
" ginal compact, between the King and Peo-
" ple.; and having violated the fundamen.
" tal laws, and withdrawn himfelf from the
" kingdom, had abdicated the government."
They ftate all their grievances, and the enor-
mities of King *James*, as their juftification;
and conclude, " Having therefore an entire
" confidence that the *Prince* of *Orange* will
" perfect the deliverance fo far advanced by
" him, and will ftill preferve them from the
" violation of their rights, which they have
" here afferted, and from all other attempts
" upon their religion, rights, and liberties."
They refolve, " that the *Prince* and *Princefs*
" of *Orange* be, and be declared King and
" Queen, *&c.* and pray them to accept the
" Crown."——In the act for declaring the
rights and liberties of the fubject [2d. Seff.
1ft W. & M.] notice is taken, that the late
King *James* did endeavour to fubvert and
extirpate the Proteftant religion, and the
laws and liberties of the kingdom; and the
particular inftances are fet forth. It then
declares, that that unhappy Prince had abdicated

cated the government; and " that it pleafed
" Almighty God, to make the *Prince* of *Orange*
" the glorious inftrument, of delivering the
" kingdom from popery and arbitrary power."
By another act a particular form of prayer is
appointed, to thank God for this deliverance;
and an act for preventing vexatious fuits
againft fuch as acted in order to the bring-
ing in their Majefties, or for their fervice,
[1ft W. & M. 2d Seff.] takes notice, " that
" at the time of his Majefty's glorious enter-
" prize for delivering this kingdom from
" Popery and arbitrary power, divers Lords
" and Gentlemen, &c. did act as lieutenants,
" &c. tho' not fufficiently authorifed there-
" unto; and did apprehend and put in cuf-
" tody divers criminous and fufpected per-
" fons; and did feize and ufe divers horfes,
" arms, and other things; and enter the
" houfes and poffeffions of feveral perfons,
" and did quarter and caufe to be quartered
" foldiers and others there; which proceed-
" ings *in times of peace and common fafety would*
" *not have been warrantable;*"—yet that act
declares, " they were neceffary, in regard
" of the exigence of public affairs, and ought
" to be juftified."

The proclamation which iffued on the ac-
ceptance of the crown by *William* and *Mary*,
is fo remarkable, that I cannot pafs it over
in filence. " Whereas it hath pleafed Al-
" mighty God, in his great mercy to this
" king-

" kingdom, to vouchfafe us *miraculous deli-*
" *verance* from Popery and arbitrary power;
" and that our prefervation is due, next un-
" der God, to the refolution and conduct of
" his Highnefs the Prince of *Orange*, whom
" God hath chofen to be the glorious inftru-
" ment, of fuch ineftimable happinefs, to
" us and our pofterity, &c. We therefore,
" the Lords fpiritual and temporal, and
" Commons, *together with the Lord Mayor*
" *and Citizens of London,* and *others of the*
" *Commons of this realm,* do *with* a full
" confent publifh and declare, &c. &c."

From thefe quotations two inferences do
moft plainly follow: firft, that the Convention of 1688 grounded their authority, and
juftified their interference, not on any ufual
powers incident to *Parliament,* in the common courfe of the conftitution; but, as I
have already faid, and cannot too often
repeat, on the peculiar neceffity of the Crifis,
on the violation of the original compact between the King and the people. Second,
that the Convention did not claim their
rights of interfering, to fill the vacant
throne, as being the two *eftates of Parliament,*
merely, but, as being the beft form of a *National Convention,* which the fhortnefs of the
time would allow, or could be got together,
on the fpur of the occafion ; and this I think,
is manifeft from their wording of the proclamation, and joining with themfelves the

Lord

Lord Mayor, and Citizens of London, and others of the Commons of England. I hope I shall be excused, for dwelling so long on this subject, considering how much the principles of the *Revolution* have been distorted, and the precedent misapplied.

Under the usual forms, in the ordinary course of the constitution, the two Houses of Parliament have no right to dispose of the executive power; neither abstract legal reasoning, nor antient precedent supports the claim. An extraordinary interference, then, can only be justified by necessity, which resolves government to its elements, and turns back the stream of power to the people. A necessity paramount the constitution can never be alledged, while the constitution remains. Is the constitution destroyed, the execution of the laws suspended, the established religion endangered by the indisposition of his Majesty?—But supposing that such a necessity did exist, and that, by any means, the throne were vacant; not the two Houses of *Parliament*, but a National Convention alone will satisfy the spirits of the maxim, which derives all power from the people.

But I will suppose it possible, that a necessity might authorise the interference of the legislative body, without dissolving the constitution. That necessity must be either the impossibility of providing for the emergency, by any other mode; or the mischief attending

attending the proposed alternative. Where an option remains no necessity can properly be said to exist. If we can provide for the emergence of the King's disability, under the forms of the constitution; it is not free and open for us to resort to the plea of necessity, for an unconstitutional interference of the legislative body. All violent and extraordinary modes of proceeding should, like *drastic* medicines, be reserved for an extremity; for they always exhaust and weaken the constitution, cause agonizing convulsions, and often death.

How then has the constitution provided for the melancholy event before us? I say by an obvious analogy between this disability, which is a temporary political death, and the actual demise of the Sovereign : and as his Heir Apparent succeeds of course on his actual demise, and is King before coronation, the next moment after the death of his ancestor, because by *the law of England there is no interregnum, and coronation is but an ornament or solemnity of honour ;* * so by a parity of state reason, and constitutional principle, in order to avoid the anarchy and discord that are to be apprehended, when there is a competition for the supreme power, the weakness and party rage incident to an effective Government ; the Heir Apparent

---

* Coke 3d. inst. Ch. i. p. 7. Hale, P. C. vol. i. p. 101.·

ought

ought to fucceed to the functions of the Sovereign; fhould the exercife of the fupreme power be fufpended, by ficknefs. Is there in this any thing difficult, abfurd, or repugnant to any one principle of law or conftitution? The doctrine of lineal hereditary fucceffion implies it; the Britifh conftitution requires it; for it abhors any chafm or ceffation of the executive power, any interpofition of extraneous authority. The maxim, that *the King never dies*, means that none of thofe cafualties, which are incident to human nature, fufpend for a moment the functions of the chief magiftrate; but that they are inftantly fupplied by the next in right of fucceffion, and the fpirit of the maxim applies to a *political* as well as *actual* demife.

Mr. *Pitt*, while he in terms afferts, *that any other fubject has an equal right to the Regency, with the Prince of Wales;* does in fact admit, that he, and he alone, as Heir Apparent, has an exclufive and indefeafible right to the exercife of the executive power; for he does admit him to be the moft proper perfon to be appointed *Regent.*—But how moft proper?—not, certainly from his character and talents; elfe, why the bafe and unworthy jealoufy? why the libellous and unconftitutional reftrictions.—It muft be then fome thing refulting from his ftation and place; fomething incident to his birth. It muft be his quality of Heir Apparent, giving him an original, inherent right, which the two Houfes of Parliament may *recognize*, but can neither *give or take away*. Here we confefs the facred voice of truth, forcing its way, through all the fimulation and deceit, of in-tereft and ambition; amidft the wild abfur-dities of faction, this confeffion is extorted *that the Prince of Wales is the moft proper per-fon to be Regent*; Words which uttered by thofe who grieve to fee, and have done their utmoft to defeat his title, can only mean, that he has an *exclufive right to be Regent*.

But we are told *Nemo eft Heres viventis*, a technical rule refulting from the feudal origin of our laws, and fuperfeded frequent-ly even in the difpofition of private proper-ty, by the liberality of modern determinati-ons. This maxim cannot be applied on this occafion, without confounding the perfon, with the political character.

The King of England has an heir during his life. The law recognizes him, the fta-tute of treafons (25 E. III) holds him forth to view as the object of peculiar veneration, marked out by the Conftitution, diftinguifh-ed from other fubjects by peculiar privi-leges; his exiftence is confidered as infepara-bly connected with the welfare of the State, and the compaffing his death is made equal-ly criminal, with the compaffing that of the King : and why ? becaufe, though not ac-tually invefted with the executive power,

G   he

he is conceived to ftand fo immediately near
it, that the moment the King is removed,
it refts on him without paufe or chafm.
He accompanies the King in the orb of his
miniftry ; an inferior luminary indeed, but
infeparably connected, and forming a part
of the fyftem, fhining with a portion of the
light of Majefty, affociated in the gratitude
and adoration of thofe who are warmed and
cheared by its influence : and the moment
the great luminary declines fucceeding to
his ftation and difpenfing his light.

But perhaps fuch mifchiefs would refult
from this doctrine, were it followed up in
practice, that it becomes neceffary for the
legiflative body by, an extraordinary interference, to difpofe of the executive power.
What are the apprehended mifchiefs ? They
can only relate to the rights and prerogatives of the Sovereign, to the power and principles of Parliament, or to the rights of the
people. Of the former, I fhall fpeak, when
I come to confider the propofed limitations.
As to the latter, it might be urged, with
equal reafon, that the two eftates of Parliament ought to interfere on the actual demife
of the King, to hold the royal functions fufpended, to fcrutinize the claim of his fuc-
ceffor, circumfcribe his authority, and fetter him with conditions. Even fuppofing
the *Heir Apparent* were immediately to affume the exercife of the executive power,
on

on the difability of the Sovereign, *that*, would no more trench on any of the confitutional rights and powers in the State, than his immediate fucceffion in cafe of an actual demife. The power of a Regency is naturally feeble; there is little danger therefore, to fear encroachments on the Conftitution, from its adminiftration of the executive power. Should any fuch thing be attempted, the legiflative body have the fame remedy againft a *Regent*, that they have againft the *King* himfelf. The remedy is not by confounding the *legiflative*, with the *execu. tive*; nor by appointing or controuling the chief magiftrate of the State; but, by precluding or correcting the abufe of his autho. rity, in the mode which the Conftitution has pointed out; by the power of impeaching his fervants and advifers; and by withhold. ing the fupplies. Thofe, who would feek for any other fecurity of our rights, feek what is unknown to the *Britifh Conftitution*, and overthrow what they would feem moft zealous to maintain.

Nothing which has been here advanced, militates with the Statute of Anne 6. c. 7, or infinuates a doubt of the power of the *whole legiflature* co-jointly, to limit and alter fucceffion. I look on the line of hereditary fucceffion, not as a thing unchangeable and indefeafible, but as a great rule of political convenience, founded in confummate wif-

dom,

dom, and fanctified by uniform practice with a few deviations, which rather strengthen the rule. I would hold it facred, I would not allow myself to suppose in speculation the possibility of breaking through it, inasmuch as any departure from it, is so dangerous, and can only be justified by some invincible necessity; no less, indeed, than the prefervation, or perdition of our present happy Constitution.

Enough has already been said on this particular point, to satisfy any man of common fenfe. But the form of the Constitution has been fo difguifed; fuch falfe and pernicious doctrines have gone abroad, fuch groundlefs clamours have been raifed, the public mind fo poifoned by illegal notions, diligently inftilled by a defperate and difhoneft faction, and greedily fwallowed by a deluded populace; that one cannot be too folicitous, to refcue and vindicate the truth, and place the right of the Heir Apparent on its true Conftitutional bafe.

There is a point of view, in which, if we confider this fubject, the right of the Heir Apparent to the perfonal exercife of the executive power, on the difability by indifpofition of the reigning Sovereign, muft appear unqueftionable. The fupreme executive power can never be annihilated, or fufpended; it is co-exiftent with the laws of nature, and the rights of man; with the

principles

principles of felf-prefervation, and the exercife of free will. The people cannot ceafe to
defire their own good ; and forms of government are but modes of purfuing the common good agreed on by the people. The
executive power muft then be fomewhere,
it is the inherent endeavour of the community at felf-prefervation. It muft be either
in the King—in his regal line—in the
legiflative body—or in the body of the
people at large. It is not in the King,
that is acknowledged.—It cannot be in the
legiflative body, the law and Conftitution of
England forbids, while it precludes an union
of the executive and legiflative power. Is
it then, in the body of the people at large ?
There is an unerring teft, by which it may
be known and afcertained, whether the
power has reverted to its original fource—
the people ; the people, who are paramount the forms of the Conftitution, might
direct it into other channels, alter its form
and defignation, in other words, new-model
the Conftitution. But will any one maintain the enormous pofition, that in cafe of a
temporary indifpofition of the Sovereign, it
is free for, or competent to the people, to
alter the Conftitution ? The power, then,
is not in the King—it is not in the legiflative body—it is not in the people. Where
fhall we look for it ? The fettlement of the
crown, which gave the executive power to
the

the firft King of the reigning family, his
heirs, and fucceffors, will tell us ;—in
them it muft remain, until fome event fhall
happen, fuch as an extinction, (which God
forbid) of the whole illuftrious line, and all
that are entitled after them, in order of fucceffion, or what is equally improbable, a
violation of the original compact; to reveft
the power in the people.

If then, the perfonal exercife of the executive power, is prevented in the King
himfelf, by any caufe ; if it cannot be inter-
rupted for a moment ; if it is an effential
element of government, and like the elements of nature, may be altered and tranf-
ferred, but cannot be deftroyed ; if it cannot
reft in the *legiflative* ; if it is manifeft, that
it has not reverted to the people, it follows,
by an inevitable confequence, that it muft re-
fide in the *Heir of the Crown, and in him
alone.* This feems to be a very plain, and
uncontrovertible truth, yet on the denial of
it, plain as it is, Mr. *Pitt,* fuch is the force
of popular delufion, builds a name as cham-
pion of the Conftitution.

I come now, to Mr. Pitt's 3d. refolution,
and waving all critical obfervations, on the
loofe ambiguous manner in which, this, as
well as the preceding one, is worded; I muft
obferve, that this refolution is not fupported
by the 2d ; for though it might (which I deny) be conceded, that it is the *right* and *duty*
of

of the *Lords* and *Commons*, to provide for the deficiencies of the executive power ; it does not follow, that the mode here alluded to, is legal or conftitutional.

And firft, I deny, that in order to preferve the King's authority entire, it is *necef-fary* for the two eftates of Parliament, to interfere. Next I affirm, that fuch an interference, as is propofed, fo far from preferving, would fubvert the King's authority.

The King's authority, in the *legal*, and that fhould be the only *parliamentary* fenfe of the words, means not the authority of the *individual*, but of the crown ; not of *Caius* or *Lucius*, but of the chief magiftrate. The law of *England* knows not the King, his people know him not, as an *individual* acting for his private emolument ; they know him, as, at once the *father* and the *creature* of his people, acting only for the public good. Every attempt, to confider the *man*, as contra diftinguifhed from the *King*, is treafon againft the Conftitution ; and can only be urged, at this time of day, by thofe who would invade the neceffary conftitutional prerogatives, and inherent functions and powers of the crown ; under the thin pretence of fecuring the poffeffion of them to his majefty. To preferve entire the authority of the King ; the two Houfes of Parliament are to take it entirely to themfelves ; the influence of the crown is to be turned againft itfelf ;

itfelf; and a minifter's gratitude to his mafter, fhown in outrage to his family.

" It is neceffary (fays this refolution) that
" the Lords and Commons fhould deter-
" mine, on the means whereby the royal
" affent may be given to bills, refpecting
" the exercife of the powers and authorities
" of the crown, in the name, and on the
" behalf of the King, during his Majefty's
" indifpofition." Is not this an exercife of
both legiflative and executive power at once,
by two eftates of Parliament, under cover
of the moft wretched fiction that ever in.
fulted the underftandings of the people.
The Lords and Commons determine on certain acts; and to give thefe acts the form of
law, without the fubftance, the fanction of the
third eftate; they fet up an airy phantom,
a Pageant created by themfelves, to perfonate
the King; they agree that it fhall be called
the third eftate, and give the royal affent,
in a manner dictated by themfelves, to acts
framed by themfelves. A rare device,
which followed up to its principle would
lead to the eftablifhment of a tyranny in
England; while, by a political legerdemain,
by the factious ufe of two or three figures in
mafquerade, a *Convention* transfers to itfelf,
all the authority of the Sovereign.

The fhadow which is fet up, to perfonate
the King, and give the royal affent to acts
or ordinances of the two Houfes of Parliament,

ment, is irreconcileable with the letter, and the fpirit of the law, it will virtually re-peal this declaratory act of Charles II. † It wants the conftitutional controul, the nega-tive, in which the fafety of the executive power confifts. The circumftance, and the only circumftance, for which the concur-rence of the King is required, to give vali-dity to acts of Parliament, is free-will, the power of pronouncing thofe emphatic words, Le Roi S'Avisera. If the King himfelf were always obliged to affent to the acts of the two Houfes, his appearance in Parlia-ment would be a very filly pageant; his con-currence in acts of legiflation, a very idle ceremony.

The object, too, for which the fiction is adopted, is fuch, as renders the precedent truly formidable.——It is for the profeffed purpofe, of paffing bills refpecting the power and authority of the crown. "The legifla-"tive (fays Blackftone) cannot abridge the "executive of any rights which it now has "by law, without its own confent. Since ". the law muft perpetually ftand as it now "does unlefs all the powers will agree to "alter it." * By means of the fiction before

---

† That ftatute did not introduce any new law; it did not declare any new principle; it only folemnly recog-nized an old maxim of law and conftitution. It was en-acted then, as a fort of *amendi honorable* of Parliament for its tranfgreffion; a memorial of their repentance of a fran-tic ufurpation.

* Comm. v. i.

us, the two Houſes of Parliament, not only
legiſlate, without the concurrence of the executive power; but the very executive power
itſelf is to be the ſubject of their legiſlation;
the victim rather of their uſurpation; while
they arrogate to themſelves a right of declaring and defining the extent, and pre-
ſcribing the exerciſe of the powers and authorities of the Crown. The words of this
reſolution are broad and general indeed.——
Under it, the two Houſes of *Parliament* may
new-model the conſtitution; abridge or re-
ſtrain the powers of the Crown; or transfer
them wholly to themſelves. All theſe acts
may come under the deſcription of bills reſpecting the power and authority of the
Crown.

Lord Coke has been quoted * as an authority in this caſe; where, in 4th Inſt. he
lays it down, that the King may be repre-
ſented by commiſſion under the great ſeal of
England, to certain Lords of Parliament, he
being within the realm, by reaſon of SOME
INFIRMITY. But this muſt be underſtood
of ſome infirmity, which leaves the King the
uſe of his faculties, the power of volition; not
a profeſſed diſability. Shall a decided incapacity to govern be eſtabliſhed by proofs; and
yet, ſhall he be ſuppoſed to do an act which
neceſſarily implies in him a full capacity?——

* See 4 Inſt. 6. and the precedents there quoted from
the Parliament-roll. 24 Edw. III. 25 Edw. III. 3. Edw.
IV. and like patent to E. of Warwick, ſame Parliament.-
So 28 Eliz.

How

How grofs an abfurdity! The King's fign
manual is requifite, as an authority for making out fuch a commiffion; and in all the
precedents, the particular caufes that oc-
cur to prevent the King's attendance, are
ftated; the King, fpeaking in his proper
perfon, recites them. Conformably then to
all the precedents, the King muft fpeak in
his own perfon, he muft recite the caufe of
his abfence—fhall he miftate the fact? That
would be error and invalidate the inftrument. Shall he ftate his own difability? His
own derangement of mind inducing an incapacity? *That*, no man is competent to
do, fays the law of the land. His Majefty's
infirmity has been compared to the cafe of
infancy; what is the precedent from the reign
of Henry VI.? An act of indemnity was
thought neceffary for the fafety of thofe who
advifed the putting of the great feal into
the hands of an infant King. Tho' the act
was the appointment of a Regent, a neceffary meafure.

But thefe commiffioners will differ widely,
from any that we find, in any precedent.
The commiffioners, in all the precedents, are
to fpeak the fenfe of the King to his Parliament; the commiffioners here, are to *eccho*
back to a parliamentary *convention their own
fenfe*. But what authority have the commiffioners under fuch a commiffion? Surely a
delegated one; Can the ftream rife above its
fource? Can the delegated authority rife

above

above its original? Can the King communicate a power which he himself does not possess? But the King himself has no power; it is confessed he has not. The want of it is the very foundation of the interference of the Lords and Commons. Does the affixing of the great seal to their commission convey to them any additional authority? by no means. The affixing of the great seal is not the appointment; the appointment must be by the King. The great seal is only affixed, in evidence of that appointment, and the authority for affixing it is the King's signature. So that, either the King must be competent to act, and then the commission is unnecessary; or incompetent, and then the commission is illegal and invalid.

But the authority of Parliament will give to this instrument that validity, which it ought to derive from the appointment of the King. Observe here, I beseech you, how the *convention* of Parliament not only reasons, but acts, in a circle, and ends where it begun. It acts, to legislate, and legislates to act. It confesses itself incompetent to the work of legislation, because of the deficiency of the executive power; and yet, the means which it adopts to supply that deficiency, are a very strong and marked act of legislation; an attempt to avoid the semblance, by usurping the reality. The impowering certain persons to do certain acts respecting

specting the community; the impowering
certain perfons to act in the name, and on
behalf of the King, in matters vitally affect-
ing his prerogative ; the directing a certain
use to be made of the great seal; surely,
these are acts of *legislation* of the most decided kind; and the only use of proceeding
in this circuitous and complicated manner,
is to dazzle and perplex the vulgar, ever ready to admire what they do not understand ;
that they may not see the enormity of the
precedent before them.

The Solicitor General of *England*, tells us,
this is a subject perplexed with difficulties,
and involved in labyrinths. It is only so, to
those who delight in crooked ways, and be-
wilder themselves, in labyrinths of their
own making. And what a clue does he offer us ! We *are to be governed by the subtleties*
of *metaphysical Lawyers*. We are to believe
in a transubstantiation more extraordinary
than any thing of Lord *Peter's* in the Tale of
a Tub, and this faith is to save the soul of
the constitution alive; but we have not so
learned the constitution. The constitution is
founded in the common sense, and common
feelings of mankind—its great truths are
simple and obvious, that he that runs may
read. Its proceedings are conformable to
its maxims; direct, dignified, and intelligi-
ble.

Mr

The Solicitor General of England, with the narrow technical reading of his profession, has adverted to legal fictions. But where are those fictions admitted? In the practice of the courts; in the offices of clerks in those courts; in the transfer of private property; and the forms and titles of judicial proceedings. Legal fictions there are, but where will he find a precedent of a conftitutional fiction. Legal fictions are fometimes admitted, not of neceffity, but merely from a religious veneration for antient forms. Thus the King is at this day fuppofed to be perfonally prefent in the Court of King's Bench, which in antient times was actually the cafe. Sometimes they are adopted, to further juftice; by amplifying the jurifdiction of courts, giving the party a more efficacious remedy, or the choice of tribunals; thus are perfons fuppofed to be in the cuftody of the marfhal, to give jurifdiction to the King's Bench; and fuch is the ftring of fictions, on which the modern proceedings in ejectment are founded; fometimes they are employed in conveyance; thus a *recovery*, under the form of an adverfe fuit, becomes one of the common affurances of the land; fometimes they are introduced for the fake of preferving uniformity of ftyle in the public acts and records; thus, though the King may be an infant,

infant, the public acts, writs, letters patent, and commiffions run in his name; and he is in that refpect fuppofed competent to all the functions of his royal ftation; but this is to avoid the infinite perplexity, and confufion, which would be introduced into public tranfactions if their titles were to be perpetually varying. In fact, legal fictions exift only in the modes and accidents; they cannot be admitted in the fubftances; that is to fay, they cannot alter the nature of things; though they may vary and regulate the manner of proceeding with refpect to them. Legal fictions therefore cannot be legal titles. They cannot in themfelves found a right or confer a property; though they may be inftrumental, in the har ds of the law, to defend or purfue that right; to recover or transfer that property. Legal fictions are the fubfervient creatures of the law, liable to be controuled, examined, fufpended, or wholly fuperfeded by it for the fake of fubftantial juftice. For it is a maxim of the law that legal fictions cannot work a wrong. Fictions of law, therefore, can never be above the law, by which they are examinable; therefore they never can be the grounds of legiflation; for then, they would be above the law. But by the mode of argument before us a legal fiction, would afcend from mere forms (its proper fphere) to fubftance. It would create a right, the moft important, the right of legiflation;

giflation ; it would repeal not only the law, but the Conftitution of the land. It would annul one of the orders of the State, and transfer all the powers to another.

It is faid letters patent, and public acts paffed even in the reign of a baby King, bear his name, and appear throughout, as if they owed their exiftence folely to him. This only fhows that the *Britifh* law abhors the appearance of any chafm, in the fupreme executive power ; and rather than fuppofe any fuch thing adopts a fiction. But in truth, as I already obferved, this fiction is only in recitals and words, confined to a department merely official and clerical, and admitted only, for the fake of uniformity in ftyle. It is no argument, to prove, that the baby King can be made to perform any kingly function, or exercife any act of him-felf, or that his royal powers and authorities may be transferred to the two Houfes of Parliament by a fiction. The fiction is au-thorifed, by the King's actual functions be-ing performed by a Regent ; but a fiction cannot give the power of appointing one. And this is confirmed by the precedent from the reign of Henry VI. Strange ! that a fiction which was only admitted to preferve entire the royal functions and authority, fhould be ufed as an argument to fubvert them.

The

The Fallacy arifes from confounding the twofold exiftence of the King. He has a po-, litical exiftence, in which the law fees in him, no difability, no infirmity, no morta, lity ; and a perfonal exiftence. It is to his political exiftence, that fictions in law ap- ply. Thus it is faid the King never dies, the King can do no wrong. The ftyle of the court of King's Bench, is, *before us at Weftminfter* ; *before us at Dublin* : for though he cannot be in two places at once ; and it would be highly improper, and interrupt the due adminiftration of juftice, fhould the King be actually and perfonally in court, at the determination of any caufe, particu- larly on the crown fide ; yet he is politically prefent by his judges. But there are certain exertions of the fupreme executive power, which are perfonal ; certain functions, in which the King muft come forward, in his natural capacity ; becaufe he muft delibe- rate ; he muft judge for himfelf, he muft ex-, ercife free-will. Such is the giving the royal affent, or diffent, to acts of the two houfes; the paffing of commiffions, letters patent, grants and pardons under the great feal. In all fuch cafes, the King's concurrence muft be fignified by fome corporeal act ; and if the Sovereign, from whatever caufe, is in- competent to fuch corporeal acts of Sove- reignty ; the perfonal exercife of the fu- preme executive power, muft be performed

I   by

by a fubftitute; but no fiction of law can make the King himfelf appoint that fub-ftitute, and fupply the deficiency of his own free-will, by an actual exercife of it. No om-nipotence of Parliament can make the people believe, at one and the fame inftant, the ac-tual ability and difability of the Sovereign.

But it is faid the mere affixing of the great feal to the commiffion, will give it the authority of a record, and legalize all fubfequent proceedings. I muft beg leave, to controvert this pofition. The authority given to inftruments under the great feal, is from their coming in the ordinary courfe of the Conftitution, according to certain eftablifhed forms, and attended with the fanction of thofe, who are invefted with le-gal official powers to iffue them, and give them validity. It is not, becaufe fuch, or fuch an inftrument happens to have the great feal affixed to it, that it has the authority of a record. The great feal muft be affixed, by thofe who have a legal right to the cuf-tody of it; it muft be affixed according to legal forms, and the import of the inftru-ment muft be legal and conftitutional. Be-fore we admit, that the great feal affixed by the command of a *Convention* of Parlia-ment, to a certain inftrument appointing fubftitutes for the King, to meet the faid Convention; and in his name, and on his behalf to affent to their acts, will have the
authority

authority of a record, and legalize all fub, fequent proceedings; we muft eftablifh, firft the authority of the Lords and Commóns, to direct fuch an application of the great feal, without the authority of the King's fign manual; and next the legality of fuch an inftrument.

According to the argument, in fupport of the propofed fiction, if any man, no matter how, becomes poffeffed of the great feal, and affixes it to any inftrument, that inftrument can no longer be queftioned; though it were a pardon to himfelf of the very offence of ftealing it. Suppofe *Blood*, inftead of the crown, had taken the great feal, or that the thieves who robbed the prefent Lord Chancellor of *England*, had ftolen the feal, and affixed it to the grant of fome patent employment, or crown lands; would the validity of fuch a grant be unqueftionable?

If the Lords and Commons have a right to direct the great feal, to be affixed to any inftrument; they muft, of courfe, have a right to grant the cuftody of it; the former would be nugatory without the latter; for the perfon having the cuftody of it, might refufe to obey them, and if they have a right to appoint a Lord Keeper, or put the great in commiffion, by a parity of reafoning they muft have a right to appoint all the other officers of State. A right inconfiftent with the known prerogatives of the crown.

But

But fuppofe the great feal legally affixed; does that preclude all further examination, fo as to fanctify, at once, what is illegal and erroneous? fuppofe it were poffible, for a commiffion to pafs the great feal empowering certain perfons, to kill all the travellers, who fhould take a certain road ; would that legalize all fubfequent proceedings? Even when the King's patents have paft the great feal, in the due courfe of law, and according to the forms of the Conftitution; they may be examined and avoided ; if any perfon is wronged by them ; if the fubject matter of them is illegal ; if they are founded on any falfe recital, or mifreprefentation of fact. For in fuch cafes the law prefumes that the King was deceived in his grant. The court of Chancery has jurifdiction, to hold plea of *fcire facias*, for the repeal of letters patent, at the fuit of a former patentee, when they are granted to feveral perfons, for one and the fame thing. But when they are againft law, or founded on a falfe fuggeftion, the King may have a Scire Facias to repeal his own grant, by letters patent. * [See c. 18, H. VI. c. 1, 3. Ed. VI. c. 4, 13 Eliz. c. 6, Eng. fiat.] And the Chancellor is fuppofed by fome antiquarians, to derive his name from cancelling letters patent. Thus we fee, that, on legal principles; the affixing

* 4 Inft. 79, 81, 82, 87, 88.

of

of the great feal, leaves the matter juft where it was. Tis a folemn evidence, of the King's concurrence in certain acts, but cannot fuperfede the neceffity of referring to, and confulting the King, by becoming that concurrence itfelf.

I proceed now to confider the propofed reftrictions, on the power of the Regent. The fpeculative doctrines contained in Mr. *Pitt's* propofitions were brought forward, not as mere declarations of a naked right ; but as the bafis of a fyftem, as a prelude to the propofed limitations. Unlefs it were firft eftablifhed that Parliament had a right to appoint a Regent it could not be maintained that they had a right to limit and prefcribe his powers; fo that the world will judge, with what fairnefs and candour Mr. *Pitt* afferted that the difcuffion of this neceffary poftulate of his own doctrine was rendered neceffary, by fuppofed declarations of the Prince's friends; declarations which were afterwards pofitively difavowed.

If the claim of the right to appoint a Regent by a Parliamentary Convention, is alarming and dangerous to the Conftitution : much more fo is it, when enforced and extended, by the exercife of a controul over his actions. That indeed, will render the executive power no longer the colleague but the pupil or fervant of Parliament; and quickly veft a complete tyranny in the *Lords* and *Commons.*

Commons. The Regent ſtands in the place of
King, and repreſents his power; by the
Conſtitution the two characters cannot be
diſtinguiſhed. Every argument, that would
now beſtow on a *Convention* the power, of
impoſing limitations on a Regent, may be
applied, at a future day, to the caſe of the
King himſelf. There might at ſome time
or other, be more plauſible arguments ad-
duced, for ſuch an interference in the caſe
of a King, than any that could be applied
to that of a Regent; for inſtance, the uncertainty of a King's health ; the probability
of a ſudden relapſe into ſome violent mala-
dy; ſuch an event would be as poſſible and
as fatal to the intereſts of the ſtate, as any
uſurpation that could be apprehended from
a Regent.

But this claim becomes yet more alarming
when we conſider the new and unprecedented
language, the bold, and diſreſpectful inſi-
nuations, which when honeſtly interpreted,
however, mean but this ; that the Heir Ap
parent of the crown ſhall be inſulted, ſhall
be deprived of his Birth-right, ſhall ſee the
prerogatives of the crown violated, its rights
invaded, and the very ſecurity of his family
on the throne aſſailed; unleſs he will ſur-
render at diſcretion, and throw himſelf on
the mercy of a faction. In addition to the
injuſtice, I ſhall barely obſerve the impro
priety of ſhowing any want of confidence
in

in the Prince, at the very moment, when all parties are agreed that he and he only ought, and fhould become the fubftitute for his royal Father; and furely the admirable conduct and temper of his Royal Highnefs on the prefent trying juncture, fhew him worthy of the utmoft confidence of the people.

A Regent during a temporary indifpofition cannot be formidable; the probability of his Majefty's fpeedy recovery, which has been urged as an argument for limiting the power of the Regent, goes ftrongly to fhew, that all limitation is wholly unneceffary. The fhorter time the Regency is likely to continue, the lefs danger is to be apprehended from any abufe of his powers by the Regent. He will not have time to entrench and fortify himfelf in the poffeffion of his authority. He will look forward to the day, when he fhall return into the mafs of the people; and will not be very anxious for the extenfion of a power which is fo foon to terminate. Befides, there will be a divifion of interefts; a number of people will look onward, to the expiration of his authority; to a courfe of things in their former channels. Should any innovation take place, the day is at hand when his minifters and advifers fhall ftand before the tribunal of Parliament. Should any thing not meet the approbation of the Sovereign, it may eafily be rectified reftified when he comes to reaffume his power.

But the argument againft intrufting the Prince with the power neceffary for the due adminiftration of government, becaufe peradventure he may abufe them, fcarcely deferves a ferious anfwer. Such a mode of reafoning, if reafoning it can be called, would go to deprive us of whatever is moft ufeful in nature, and eftimable in fociety. The moft nourifhing aliments, the moft wholefome beverages, may be converted to poifon when taken in excefs. Even the beft and moft perfect forms of government have been abufed and made the engines of violence and wrong. The liberties of the people have degenerated into licentioufnefs. The pureft fyftems of religion, the difpenfations of Deity itfelf have been made the pretext of perfecution and cruelty. Yet, fhall we, for this, fubvert civil order, abolifh liberty, and blafpheme Heaven? ·

The authority of a Regent is too often feeble; his conduct is generally marked by caution and diffidence. He has not the fame power of extending his influence, and attaching followers, as a King. His condefcenfions are lefs flattering, his favours lefs ennobling, his refentments lefs awful. Such, in general, is the condition of a Regent.— Now when a ftrong adminiftration is required, when the affairs of *Europe* are in fuch a
                                    complicated

complicated fituation, and *Britain* in the greateft danger of being involved in a war. Is this a time to enfeeble inftead of ftrengthin g the hands of the executive power.

Do thofe who would deprive government of its vital force and energy, fetter the genuis, and cramp the refources, proftrate the dignity, and perhaps endanger the falvation of the *Britifh* Empire, to gratify their own fpleen, or provide for themfelves a return to ftation and emolument; do they deferve the applaufes which have been lavifhed on them by the multitude?

It cannot be thought or fuppofed, and therefore would not, I fhould hope, be infinuated, that any particular interference of Parliament is neceffary, to fecure to his Majefty the full exercife of his royal authority, whenever his indifpofition fhall happily be removed. The fuppofition of any fuch neceffity is an atrocious libel on his Royal Highnefs the *Prince of Wales.* It does no lefs, than call in queftion the filial Duty, the Loyalty, the Patriotifm, the Juftice, and the good fenfe of that exalted Perfonage. *Is not the King's eldeſt ſon, the Heir Apparent of his kingdom,* (as is juftly expreft in that admirable letter of a great Perfonage) *the perſon moſt bound to the maintenance of his Majeſty's juſt prerogatives and authority, as well as moſt intereſted in the happineſs, the proſperity, and the glory of his people?* Let us

hear

hear no more of a foul infinuation, too abfurd and groundlefs to be fwallowed by the
meaneft of the rabble.

A folicitude perfonal to his Majefty is
profeft, a defire of fparing his feelings, by
preferving every thing in the fame ftate;
fo that on his recovery from the prefent ma-
lady, there may exift as few circumftances,
as poffible, to mark the exiftence of his ill-
nefs, or recall it to his mind. Such language is unprecedented in the Englifh conftitution. What bold individual fhall dare
to feparate the interefts of the King from
the interefts of the community? fhall pro-
fefs himfelf influenced by private gratitude,
in a great public tranfaction; and avow,
without the fear of punifhment, that the
private gratification of the King, and not
the well-being of the ftate, fhall be the
rule of his conduct? And fhall the wretched deluded people call the factious individual, who does fo, the friend of the conftitution?

But fuppofing this delicacy might be com-
mendable were it real, or what it profeffes
feafible, but yet Majefty will, of neceffity,
find many things altered during his abfence,
as I may call it; the exigencies of government will require it. It is paying fo good
a King but a bad compliment, to fuppofe
that he could be gratified by finding the
interefts of his people facrificed to fuch a
point

point of delicacy ; that he would be pleafed,.
to find public affairs ill adminiftered, the
vigour and ftrength of government relaxed,
and every thing thrown into diforder, under pretence of keeping things in the fame
ftate his Majefty left them.

I appeal to the common fenfe of every
man—has Mr. *Pitt's* conduct been anfwer-
able to his profeffions? Will things be found
in the fame ftate ; fhould providence grant
his Majefty's recovery, to the prayers of his
people? furely no. He will find an af-
fumption of very great powers to the Houfes
of Lords and Commons ; ftrong decifions on
abftract queftions, that materially affect his
prerogatives, and the rights of his auguft
houfe ; and a fignal and violent precedent
of an interference of the legiflative branches,
unknown to the Conftitution. It is eafy to
judge, whether his Majefty's feelings will
be lefs wounded at all this, than at fome
alterations induced by a mere exercife of
the executive power, and regular prerogative ; in the grant of offices, the creation of
peers, or the diffolution of Parliament.

Let us now conlider the propofed limitations of the power of the Regent ; comprehending a reftriction as to the grant of pen-
fions, and offices, for life, or in reverfion;
and the creation of peers ; for with them
only, I mean to trouble my readers.

The

The power of appointing his fervants, and rewarding their fervices, feems to be neceffarily and infeparably inherent in the character of chief magiftrate ; as being abfolutely requifite to the due performance of the functions. A reftitution in this point would ve ry nearly approach the ufurpation of the long Parliament, when they drove Charles the firft, to the laft extremity, by claiming the appointment of the King's offices. Can a requeft thus reftricted, expect to be ferved zealoufly or affectionately ? But fuppofing he fhould find in the attachment and fidelity of his minifters thofe refources, which are denied by the limitation of his powers ; is it juft ? is it confiftent with the honour of a great nation, to feal up the functions of public bounty, for an unlimited time, againft merit, however diftinguifhed ? to fay to thofe who fhall fpend their talents, their fortunes, their health, and their lives, in the fervice of the State ; you muft not hope, when you fink to reft after your honourable labours, any fupport for your families from that country which you have ferved, perhaps faved by your exertions ? We know, that the offspring of the moft fplendid and difinterefted ftatefman *England* ever faw, muft have felt the ftings of penury, had not t he gratitude of their country interfered to fnatch them from diftrefs. As to the grant of reverfionary employments, there is in

that,

that, a faving to the public, a political economy ; inafmuch, as the families of thofe who have deferved well, may be provided for, by means of them, without burthening the nation, by an encreafe of the penfion lift.

Titles of honour have ever been the proper rewards of diftinguifhed merit, in the cabinet or the field. Many of the noble Lords in the Britifh Houfe of Peers, are living memorials of the high deferts, and eminent fervices, of their parents, and ancef-tors. The creation of Peers, is an undoubted flower of the crown, which cannot without disfiguring and difgracing it, be torn away. Such a meafure at the fame time, that it would be a great difcouragement to virtuous actions, to learning and induftry, and detrimental to the Houfe of Peers itfelf, by preventing fuch frequent fupplies from going into it, as the nature of fuch a body requires ; might be a means of changing the Conftitution into an *ariftocracy*, one of the worft forts of flavery. Confider, I befeech you, to what a ftate the Regent may eventually be reduced by the propofed reftriction. The Regency may by poffibility continue a long time ; fo that the power of creating peers may be expended during twenty, thirty, or forty years. And during all this time, an ariftocracy may be maintained by the confederacy of two, or three great
families,

families, which would form such a body among the Lords, as the crown would not be able to controul. And this would be facilitated by the diminution of number in the efflux of time. But there is a more immediate and preffing danger to be apprehended; at leaft, the cafe, which I fhall put, is poffible. Suppofe a majority of the House of Peers, at the devotion of an ambitious fubject, a turbulent and difcontented fpirit; thwarting the wifeft counfels, impeding the moft neceffary meafures, and confpiring to render *government difficult if not impracticable, in the hands of the perfon deflined to reprefent the King's authority.* Suppofe, a large revenue withdrawn from the interference of the Regent, and a number of offices of emolument and honour, made independent of him, and fubjected to the fole and exclufive controul of another perfon; and fuppofe all the power and influence, thus withdrawn from the fubftitute of royalty; fuppofe it conferred on a man fuch as I have defcribed, and turned by him againft the executive power; in vain fhall the chief magiftrate look for aid to the wifdom and virtue of the *Commons*; a firm *phalanx*, will be oppofed to him in the Lords, which fhall fruftrate his beft intentions, and *render it impoffible to carry on the executive government of the country.* It may be faid, this is a degree of improbable criminality, a vifionary phantom, of

atrocious

atrocious ambition ; but the profpect of the prefent.—" *A project for introducing weaknefs,* " *diforder, and infecurity in every branch of* " *the adminiftration of affairs ;—a project for* " *dividing the Royal Family ; for feparating* " *the Court from the State, and thereby disjoin-* " *ing government from its accuftomed fupport.*" All this has been perpetrated already, and may well juftify our apprehenfions for the future.

I forbear to enlarge on the two other re-ftrictions ; they muft fill every friend of the Conftitution, with indignation and forrow, as a precedent of an outrageous tearing afun-der the fupreme executive power ; that pow-er, which, in contemplation of law and con-ftitution, is *one, entire,* and *indivifible.* But they are not likely to be the fubject of much difcuffion, in this kingdom, for the meridian of which I chiefly write ; and this pamphlet has already grown upon me, to an immode-rate length ; perhaps many things in it might have been retrenched, many comprefs ; but I write on the fpur of the occafion, and hafte is generally the parent of prolixity. During the delay of correction, the moment of be-ing ufeful would pafs away, to return no more.

I proceed to fome reflections, which pe-culiarly fuggeft themfelves to the people of *Ireland.* This country ftands in a predica-ment different from that of any colonial or affociated

affociated ftate which antient or modern hif-tory can produce. It is connected with *Great Britain*, not by an union of incorporation; not by an union of fubjection and depend-ence, *that* we have happily difclaimed; nor yet by an exprefs fœderal union, no monu-ment of fuch a compact exifts; but by the unity of the executive power alone. As the executive binds together the two affemblies of Lords and Commons of the fame king-dom, in one Parliament; fo it connects two independent kingdoms in one empire. *Ire-land* and *Britain* are members of the fame body; one cannot be torn from the other, without disfiguring the exquifite beauty, per-haps endangering the vital exiftence of the whole.

Why are we told that we muft lean and hearken after the example of *Britain*; we muft adopt what has been done in the two Houfes of the Englifh Parliament?—If the *Englifh* Parliament, on the difcuffion of quef-tions which affect the very vitals of the con-ftitution, acts conformably to law, and the true fpirit of that conftitution, as declared and eftablifhed in 1688; we may, not lite-rally copy them, we may, not blindly follow them; but we fhall certainly meet and coin-cide with them; not as looking to what they may have done but adopting, I may fay, kin-dred notions not lineally derivative, but col-lateral from a common ftock.

It

It is impoſſible, indeed, that what is done in *England* ſhould be a ſtrict rule, to be ſervilely and literally adopted by *Ireland*. The ſituation of this country being very peculiar, as I have obſerved; peculiar intereſts and duties will ariſe out of that ſituation, and ſuggeſt peculiar maxims of political conduct to the people. The ſame rule, muſt govern like, not diſſimilar caſes; and as this country differs ſo widely from *Britain* in her circumſtances; it may be neceſſary, even though what was done in *Britain* might have been right, as reſpecting *Britain*, to vary from it here, when we come to conſider what the exigencies and circumſtauces of this country may ſuggeſt or demand.

There are two events of which *Iriſhmen* ſhould never loſe ſight;—The *glorious Revolution* of 1688, which finally and fully eſtabliſhed the *Britiſh* conſtitution; and the no leſs glorious *Revolution* of 1782, which made that conſtitution our own, and inveſted us with full powers not only to enjoy, but to cheriſh, to protect, and to maintain it inviolate. Theſe ſhould be the landmarks of their conduct, the one gives the end, the other the means; the one makes them men, the other freemen.——Three great objects, then, offer themſelves to the regards of *Iriſhmen;* objects which they are bound to hold faſt as their exiſtence, and defend with their beſt blood.—The connexion of this country with

L   *Great*

Great Britain;—the independency of the legiflature of Ireland ;—and the maintenance of the *Britifh* conftitution. The two firft are peculiar to ourfelves ; the laft is in common to us with every fubject of the empire; but our mode of purfuing it, may be varied by our fituation.

Of the mode of purfuing thofe objects, and the means to be employed, we alone are competent to judge. *Britain* being the more ftrong and powerful part of the empire, her interference to point out the means, or prefcribe the mode, would totally deftroy the fubftance. The greateft mifchiefs may refult to us from her meddling in our deliberations, on points of conftitution ; whereas, none can redound to her, from our keeping them free and unbiaffed by dictation or controul. Let us diveft ourfelves therefore of all filly notions, that it is neceffary to *copy here*, what has been done in *England*; notions which originate in a concealed treafon againft this country, in a lurking dereliction of the rights of *Ireland*. The mode and form of what has been done will I think be found impoffible to be adopted in *Ireland*, and the fubftance inexpedient.

Every friend to the laws, the religion, the welfare of this country, muft hold dear the connexion with *Great Britain*. Joined with her *we purfue the triumph, and partake the gale* ;—disjoined we fhould become fmall among

among the nations. Our manners, our language, the ties of blood, and the vicinity of foil all point us out as parts of the fame great empire. We form as it were a mighty arch, on which the auguft forms of Juftice, Liberty, Commerce, Opulence, and Renown ftand aloft and confpicuous to the eyes of the world. Of this arch the King the common Sovereign is the key ftone, that binds the whole together ; but the pledge of union is not the name, but the reality of King ; the actual common exercife of the executive power, giving a communication of councils and a co-operation of national force. Power diftinct from the perfonal exercife of it is nonfenfe; a King, diftinct from the exercife of his prerogative and authority, is a contradiction; a King incapable of governing is a creature which the conftitution knows not, fuch an incapacity therefore muft be a political death. It is no matter whether the executive power is in the hands of King or Regent ; we are bound together within the circle of the fame imperial crown; it is the unity of the Chief Magiftrate, and that alone, which connects the two kingdoms. Mr. *Pitt*'s doctrine, which invefts the two Houfes of Parliament, in cafe of the King's indifpofition, with a general difcretion of appointing any perfon in the kingdom Regent, tends directly to feparate the perfonal exercife of the executive power in the two countries ;

and wears away and attenuates the band of mutual affociation. Every meafure, which renders lefs fecure the lineal fucceffion; which threatens to make the throne elective; threatens alfo a diffolution of the empire into its component parts.

The two Houfes of Lords and Commons are equally independent, have equal rights and powers, in *Ireland*, with thofe which the correfpondent affemblies poffefs in *England :* Now, if we copy the example of *England*, and entertain the abftract queftion, our declarations muft be equally ftrong, or we fhall be traitors to ourfelves. It will be incumbent on us to declare, that it is the right and duty of the Lords and Commons of *Ireland*, to provide for the perfonal exercife of the exe-cutive power; but how fhall we reconcile this with the folemn act of the legiflature of this country, the act of *Recognition* of the 4*th of William* and *Mary*, which folemnly de-clares, that the executive power in the two countries fhall be one and the fame; and that *Ireland* fhall be for *ever* annexed and united to the imperial crown of *England ?—* How fhall we avoid this dilemma ?—The way is obvious ;—by declining the difcuffion, of abftract queftions big with fuch difficul-ties and mifchiefs; and purfuing the fimple, the legal, and conftitutional mode of *addrefs: ing his Royal Highnefs the Prince of Wales, and praying him to affume the Government of this Realm.*

If

If the two Houfes of Lords and Commons
in this kingdom, either do not poffefs, or
would be unwife in afferting the power of
appointing a *Regent* ; it follows, as a neceffary confequence, that they cannot entertain
any plan of reftrictions or limitations of the
power of the Regent; for the declaration of
the abftract right is a poftulate, a corner
ftone, on which the whole fyftem of reftrictions is founded ; and if you take *that* away
the fabric muft fall to the ground. Befides,
the profeffed object of the reftrictions in *England* being to fecure to his Majefty the immediate exercife of the Royal Authority, when
it fhall pleafe God to remove his indifpofition ; they are wholly unneceffary here ; his
Majefty is already perfectly fecured ; for, by
the act of recognition above mentioned, on
his refuming the adminiftration of affairs in
England, he will immediately, and *ipfo facto*,
become invefted with the executive power in
Ireland.

Now, with refpect to the independence
of the legiflature of this country. In addition to the jealoufy, which the fubjects, in
any limited monarchy, muft entertain of
the influence of the crown; the people muft
be poffeft with a well grounded apprehenfion, for it is grounded on long and fad ex-
perience, of the power, the claims, a d uf-
urpations of the *Britifh Parliament.* That
precious boon, which we refcued with dif
ficu'ty

ficulty from the reluctant grafp of oppre..
fion, we are bound to tranfmit facred and
entire to our pofterity. We are not to con-
tend merely with the ambition of a monarch,
or the corruption of his minifters; thefe are
lighter mifchiefs ; their progrefs is flow, the
forms of the conftitution remain, and preferve in themfelves the principles of purifi-
cation. Our conteft is with enemies, that
require our utmoft vigilance, and threaten
to overwhelm the conftitution at a blow;—
with the pride and prejudices of the *Britifh*
nation; with the wakeful jealoufy of commerce ; the cruel fpirit of monopoly, the il-
liberal intolerance of manufacture, and in-
veterate habits of unjuft domination. The
Britifh Parliament, rankling from our late
victory, and armed with a ftring of precedents to juftify ufurpation, waits to feize the
moment of our weaknefs and inattention,
and renew claims, which they fo reluctantly
abandoned.—What mound or barrier fhall
we oppofe to the current, which has long
fet in againft the wealth, the independence
and general profperity of this Kingdom ?
What, but the paternal care and affection of
the common fovereign, the wifdom and
firmnefs of his minifters ?

We fhould be cautious, therefore, as we
wifh well to the *Independence of Ireland*, of
admitting the principle, that the example of
the *Britifh Parliament* has any binding force,

or

or authority in this country; inſtead of copying, we ſhould be proud to diſſent from their conduct. Firſt, becauſe what has been done by them is *wrong in itſelf*; next, becauſe here is a ſolemn occaſion of diſclaiming the controul of the *Britiſh Parliament*. By diſſenting from them, in this inſtance, we ſhall give a memorial of our independence to the lateſt poſterity; an aſſertion of the right, by an exerciſe of the power, decided, unequivocal, and ſtrong, beyond a thouſand oral or written declarations.

Would it be wiſe, ye friends of *Ireland*, to ſacrifice the golden advantages of ſuch a declaration of our independence, and yield to the ſuggeſtions of intereſted men, who would drive us into a diſcuſſion of abſtract queſtions? the diſcuſſion of abſtract queſtions in *England* has been a ſtruggle for power, a trial of party ſtrength, at the expence of the conſtitution. What have we to do with the parties of *England?* we have only one party, to purſue the good of our country. And the good of our country requires, that we ſhould confer the executive power *free and unfettered on the Heir Apparent of the Crown.*

Why ſhould we conſpire to exalt the authority of the *Britiſh Parliament*, the great object of our fears, on the ruins of the executive power, the great ſource of our protection? What can we expect, when the claims

of

of the *Britiſh Legiſlature* ſhall have ſwallow-
ed up the legal powers, and conſtitutional
prerogatives of the crown; but the poor fa-
vour of being the laſt devoured?——We
have now ſuch an opportunity, as ſeldom
occurs, given us by the ſtrange and uncon-
ſtitutional cond t of Mr. *Pitt's* party in
England; we have an opportunity of concili-
ating the affections of the Heir Apparent of
the crown, by an aſſertion of our own rights.
Let us ſeize the occaſion; we may frequently
be driven to throw ourſelves on the affection, and good offices of our ſovereign; let
us now purchaſe them before hand; by
throwing *Ireland* into the ſcale of his influence; and as far as in us lies reſcuing the
executive, from the encroachments of the
legiſlative power.

It was thus the Commons of *England* roſe
to conſideration and greatneſs; the King
looked about for aid, to protect him againſt
the overweening power and rude encroachments of his Barons: He drew forth
the third eſtate of the people, from the
depths of the loweſt obſcurity; he gave them
a weight and influence in the community,
and the Commons repaid with intereſt, that
ſtrength, ſecurity, and conſequence which
they derived from the crown.—Who knows
but ſomething ſimilar may happen with re-
ſpect to *Ireland*, from a ſimilar reiprocation
of good offices?

I come

I come now to the third great object in the confideration of *Irifhmen, that,* to which the two former are fubordinate and ancillary, the maintenance of the *Britifh Conftitution,* of which we are now made partakers. And on Conftitutional principles, it is manifeft, that we cannot poffibly adopt Mr. *Pitt's* plan of providing for the temporary vacancy of the *Throne.* To give, is to legiflate, to appoint a Regent is an act of legiflation. But it is confeft that the Parliament of this kingdom wants the third component part, which is neceffary to give it legiflative validity. Mr. *Pitt's plan,* is to appoint the Regent by bill. It is impoffible on Mr. *Pitt's* principles, to give the royal affent to fuch a bill; without affenting a controul, of the *Britifh* over the *Irifh Parliament;* for the Regent, according to him, being merely the creature of the Parliament, deriving the authority, not from any thing inherent in himfelf, but folely from their appointment, his authority is, in fact, the authority of Parliament; and thus muft the *Britifh* Parliament, on Mr. *Pitt's* principles, have an affirmative, or negative, on the acts of the *Irifh* Parliament, with refpect to the Regency.

And when we fpeak of Conftitution; can it be forgotten under whofe aufpices this land was emancipated? Through whom are we enabled to debate the high and mo-

M   mentous

mentous fubjects of the prefent? Is it not through the miniftration of thofe men, who now fhare the councils, and enjoy the confidence of his Royal Highnefs the Prince of Wales? Through them, are we placed in our prefent fituation of independence : and a proud and dignified fituation it is,

Quod optanti nemo promittere Divum auederet,
Valveuda Dies en attulit ultro.

What the utmoft ftretch of enthufiaftic fpeculation could not dare to promife to the champions of *Irifh* independence, the chance of the day has brought within our grafp. We now can pay to Great Britain the full price of the boon, which we demanded from her. At this awful crifis of her fate, her Genius looks up to us with reverential anxiety, though with fifterly confidence ; fhe calls upon Ireland to defend that Conftitution which fhe had built up for us, and the bleffings of which fhe has fhared with us, againft a defperate faction, which has extinquifhed all her energy, and crufhed her adherents. At fuch a moment, can we be infenfible of our own importance? Shall we not know our own value, or refufe to be juft to ourfelves, and to the truft which we have affumed, and fworn as at the altar, to tranfmit to our defcendants.

gain

To value any blefling aright, we muft firft underftand it; What did *Irifhmen* obtain by the Revolution of 1782? What did we gain by the eloquence of our public leaders, the firmnefs of Parliament, and the exertions of the people? Was it a fhare of faction? Was it a moiety of civil difcord, a fifter's portion of cabal and anarchy? No; God forbid. It was a participation in that happy Conftitution, which is the confummate work of ages, and the boaft of human wif.dom. Was the nation pledged? Did we fo boldly pafs the *Rubicon*? to win the poor privilege of being the retainers of an *Englifh* party, the fatellites of an afpiring Minifter—the humble infruments of his ambition, to be wielded at the difcretion of a fervile delegate? No: we demanded, and we obtained a Conftitution, as it was fettled by the *bill of rights*; a Conftitution where King, Lords, and Commons, balance, controul, and fupport each other. A Conftitution which we pledged ourfelves to defend, on the principles, on which we found it ftated, while we fecured to ourfelves the power of ftanding to our pledges, and fulfilling our engagements. I cannot place this great and glorious truth in too many different lights; we are not only the guardians of our own liberties, but the guarantees of thofe of *Britain*: the *Britifh Conftitution* cannot be invaded, without fapping the foundation of our

M 2   Conftitution,

Conftitution, and every affertion of our rights, muft lend a new fecurity to thofe of *Englifhmen.*

Where then fhall we find any man, or fet of men, hardy enough to call upon us to concur in violating the Conftitution, in transferring the rights of the Sovereign to the two remaining eftates of Parliament, and confounding the executive power with the legiflative ? If a Convention in *Great Britain* hath been guilty of fuch a violence, we will fhew our attachment to that country, by diffenting from her example—we will all ftand forth, as one man, to oppofe a barrier to the invafion ; and the vital fpirits, and the warm blood of the Conftitution having circulated through *Ireland,* as an extremity, will return, to warm and cherifh *Britain,* as the heart.

The anfwer, therefore, which we have to make to thofe who tell us, that we muft fol-low the example of Britain—we *muft* adopt what has been done in the two Houfes of the *Britifh* Parliament, is this—" If the *Britifh* Parliament lofe fight of Conftitutional prin-ciples ; if it have recourfe to new maxims, and eftablifh principles deftructive of thofe, on which the Conftitution we obtained from *Britain* was founded ; we will defend them againft her Parliament ; we will read a lef-fon of Conftitution to the parent country, and

awake

awake her drooping fpirit, into a recollec-
tion of thofe days, when other councils, and
other men miniftered to her under unfore-
feen emergencies."

No, my Countrymen, in our demand
of a free Conftitution, we were not
candidates for our difgrace. If we do not
ufe that Conftitution wifely, better were it
that we had never obtained it. If it is to be
mangled and disfigured, better were it to
have remained paffive and fubfervient; to
be ftill exiled from our Birth-right, that we
might now view the unhallowed fpectacle,
at a diftance, inftead of joining in the trage-
dy. But we will, I know we will, ufe that
Conftitution wifely and tenderly; we will
yield her an afylum, when expelled from
Britain. We will fnatch her to our hearts.
We will cherifh her in our bofoms. We
will verify the words of our illuftrious coun-
tryman and patriot, in fuch a degree, that
they fhall feem to have been dictated by
the immediate influence of a patriotic fpirit.
" Admit us at once, (faid he, addreffing
" himfelf to England) into the poffeffion of
" our birth-right, the vigour of our youth
' will be the prop of your old age; give us
" the power, and the moft glorious fervice
" in which it will be our pride to employ it,
" will be in fupporting the crazy frame of
" your Conftitution." We are put in pof-

feffion

feſſion of the birth-right, we enjoy the power ; let us ſhew the ſame ſpirit that actuated
us when the prophecy was uttered, and let
our *power* be exerted in defending the *rights*
which this ſpirit ſecured to us in the day of
our triumph.

F I N I S.

www.ingramcontent.com/pod-product-compliance
Lightning Source LLC
Chambersburg PA
CBHW020028030726
47499CB00007B/2324